TEMPTING GIFTS

A Castle Mountain Lodge Romance

ELENA AITKEN

Ink Blot Communications

ISBN: 978-1-927968-75-8

Also by Elena Aitken

Castle Mountain Lodge

Unexpected Gifts

Hidden Gifts

Unexpected Endings - Short Story

Mistaken Gifts

Secret Gifts

Goodbye Gifts

Tempting Gifts

Holiday Gifts

Promised Gifts

Accidental Gifts

The Castle Mountain Lodge Collection: Books 1-3

The Castle Mountain Lodge Collection: Books 4-6

The Castle Mountain Lodge Collection: Books 7-9

The Castle Mountain Lodge Complete Collection

The Springs Series

Summer of Change

Falling Into Forever

Second Glances

Winter's Burn

Midnight Springs

She's Making A List

Summit of Desire

Summit of Seduction

Summit of Passion

Fighting For Forever

The Springs Collection: Volume 1

The Springs Collection: Volume 2

The Springs Collection: Volume 3

The Springs Complete Collection - Books 1-10

Destination Paradise

Shelter by the Sea

Escape to the Sun

Hidden in the Sand

Ever After

Choosing Happily Ever After

Needing Happily Ever After

Wanting Happily Ever After

Fighting Happily Ever After

We Wish You A Happily Ever After

Keeping Happily Ever After

Finding Happily Ever After

Seeking Happily Ever After

Cherishing Happily Ever After

Ever After: Volume One (Books 1-4)

The McCormicks

Love in the Moment

Only for a Moment

One more Moment

In this Moment

From this Moment

Our Perfect Moment

Stand Alone Stories

All We Never Knew

Drawing Free

Sugar Crash

Composing Myself

Betty & Veronica

The Escape Collection

Vegas

Nothing Stays in Vegas

Return to Vegas

Timber Creek

When We Left

When We Were Us

When We Began

When We Fell

Bears of Grizzly Ridge

His to Protect

His to Seduce

His to Claim

Hers to Take

His to Defend

His to Tame

His to Seek

Hers for the Season

Bears of Grizzly Ridge: Books 1-4

Bears of Grizzly Ridge: Books 5-8

Halfway Series

Halfway to Nowhere

Halfway in Between

Halfway to Christmas

Chapter One

LISA GIBBS WIPED a smear of blue finger paint off her cheek and then, before the little girl who sat at the miniature table across from her could squirm away, used the cloth to clean most of the paint off her smiling face. She couldn't do anything about the paint that had found its way into her hair, but it would wash out. Besides, a messy child after arts and crafts was almost always a happy child. And if her parents didn't like it when they came to pick her up from the Cub Club, well, that was too bad.

"Why don't you go play, Emily?" Lisa suggested. "I'll put your painting on the rack to dry and you can take it with you when you leave."

The little girl nodded. "It's for my mommy. I love her the mostest."

Lisa felt the familiar pinch of jealousy. Which was ridiculous because she didn't even know the little girl's mother. But it didn't matter. She didn't need to know the woman to envy her. Whoever she was, she had a beautiful little girl, and Lisa could guess she also had a husband who doted on her. The perfect family. Just like all the families who visited Castle Mountain Lodge.

Lisa watched Emily join a group of children building Lego before she cleaned up the painting supplies and returned them to the supply cupboard. She loved her job. Loved working with the children. It was their parents she had trouble with. They were all so damn perfect and happy and…the complete opposite from anything she'd ever had, or likely ever would.

The bells on the door chimed, alerting her to the arrival of a new guest. Instinctively, Lisa looked for Morgan. Her boss—and friend—was in the middle of reading a story to a small group who hung off her every word. Morgan waved at Lisa to handle the visitor and she nodded her response. Lisa grabbed the registration clipboard and turned around.

When she saw the man in front of her, tall and filling out his T-shirt with muscles that looked to be earned by many hard hours in the gym, Lisa momentarily forgot what to say. She'd certainly never seen him before. But that wasn't unusual at the Lodge. Guests were always coming and going, bringing their kids in and out of the child care center.

"Welcome to the Cub Club," she said. She gave him a bright friendly smile. "What can I help you with?" He didn't have a child with him, which was unusual. "Are you picking up your child?" She scanned the list, trying to figure out who he might be picking up. "Because I'll have to see some ID before we release them to you."

"Oh no. I'm not here to pick anyone up." She raised her eyebrows at his choice of words; he tipped his head briefly and gave her a strange look before he added, "I'm just wondering how this works here." He gestured around the room.

"Well, usually you have a child to register in the program." If he was some creeper who was just trying to figure out a way to be close to the kids, there was no way he'd be getting past her. The fact that he looked as if he could pick her up and throw her over his shoulder hardly seemed like an important detail. She forced a smile and tried to be as friendly as possible until she could figure out what he was after. "This is a club for kids, but if you're looking for something to do at the Lodge, I could direct you in the right direction. We have a wide variety of activities for our older guests as well, sir." She put her clipboard down and looked at him pointedly.

"Oh no." A smile crossed his face and he laughed as he realized what she was implying. "It's not like that at all."

Lisa's instincts were to believe him. Despite his broad chest and thick arms, he didn't look like the threatening type. In fact, he looked like the type of guy she would normally be attracted to. Very attracted. But that was before. Things were different now and a man, even one as attractive as the one who stood in front of her, was not on her agenda. "Well, how is it then, sir?"

"Jason," he said. "My name's Jason. And I actually am wondering about the Cub Club. Not for myself obviously," he added quickly.

The man crossed his arms over his chest, which drew more attention to them as far as Lisa was concerned. She tried not to stare at his defined muscles.

"Obviously." She looked directly into his big green eyes. "That would be weird."

He chuckled and nodded. "That it would. But don't worry, I'm not some kind of crazy. I actually need to register Kayden ."

"Kayden? That's a nice name."

"Yeah. His mom named him after his grandfather." There was a time, not too long ago, when Lisa would've inquired further about Kayden, his mom, and whether his extremely good-looking and charismatic father was a single father and potentially in need of a date. But that was before she almost lost everything she'd worked for at the Lodge because of her tendency to flirt, and well, more than flirt, with guests. After the Gage Mitchell incident, when she took her attraction to the movie star who was staying at the Lodge a little too far, she was lucky she still had a job at all. And there was no way she was going to make that mistake again. Things had changed. She had changed.

She glanced up from her clipboard where she'd started writing. "Okay." She returned her attention to the clipboard with the professional detachment she'd perfected since the *incident.* "We can get your son registered without a problem. How many days will you be visiting us at Castle Mountain?"

She held the pen poised in her hand and waited for his response. When he didn't say anything, she looked up. "Sir? How many days?"

"It's Jason," he said finally. Amusement laced his voice. "Remember?"

"I remember." She returned his smile. He was so disarming, she couldn't help how her body responded to him. "How many days would you like to register for, Jason?" She emphasized his name this time. "Basically, how it works is every day we plan different activities for the children so they can enjoy some fun, kid time, and you and um…Kayden's mom…"She tilted her head with the implied question that she knew she had no business asking and tried to tell herself that she didn't care what the answer was. When Jason only shrugged in response, she continued. "Well, then the two of you are free to enjoy some of the activities at the Lodge that aren't quite so child friendly, and everyone has a good time."

"Sounds good," Jason said. "I'll sign him up for the day after tomorrow."

"Great. You said your son's name was Kayden?" Lisa scribbled down the date next to his name.

"Oh, he's not my son."

His words caught her and she looked up and took a deep breath. "Okay," she said. "Your stepson then?"

Jason chuckled. Apparently he found her funny. "I never said he belonged to me. Kayden's actually my nephew. My sister's still checking in so I thought I'd come down and take care of things for her."

A flush passed over Lisa's face. She really shouldn't jump to conclusions. "I'm sorry," she said. "I just assumed. But we generally only get parents coming into the Cub Club. It was an easy mistake."

"And do you flirt with all the parents?"

"I wasn't flirting." Lisa thrust her shoulders back and crossed her arms, because the last thing she was doing or intended to do was flirt.

"Oh, really?" He grinned.

She wanted to be irritated by his grin, but it only made him more attractive and that was way too dangerous. "Absolutely not." She shook her head and narrowed her eyes into a glare.

"Well," he said with an easy smile, "if you were, I'd be flattered."

Damn it. *He* flirted with *her*.

She bit her bottom lip a little and forced any and all thoughts that were even remotely inappropriate from her head. She wasn't going to go down that road again. Not even for a man who looked like Jason. She shook her head firmly. "Sorry to disappoint, but I was just doing my job. I am definitely not interested." She emphasized the words so there'd be no further misunderstanding. And by the transformation on his face, Lisa was pretty sure he got the point. A part of her, especially the part that thought he was a nice guy, felt bad.

"If you say so."

"It's not that—"

"Hey, whatever you say." He tucked his hand in his back pocket, a move so effortlessly casual, it made Lisa's stomach flip in a way that both annoyed and excited her. "So, what else do we need to get Kayden registered?"

Lisa swallowed hard; for some unknown reason, she felt the need to explain. "Look, it's not you; it's just that I kind of make it a point not to date guests." She searched his face for an indication that he wasn't still upset with her, and she couldn't help but wonder why she cared at all. He was just a guest. He'd be gone in a few days, and as long as she behaved, she'd still have her job. It wasn't like her to care about what anyone thought, let alone some random guy she'd just met. But there was something about Jason. "Seriously. If it wasn't for that, I would totally be flirting with you." *Why on earth did she just say that?* Lisa bit the end of her pen to keep from talking any more.

His eyes flashed, and the corner of his mouth turned up in a wicked grin. "And what makes you think it was a *date* I was interested in? I had something much different in mind."

He emphasized the word date and his eyes flashed with a look Lisa had become all too familiar with when it came to men. She took an automatic step back and shook her head. Anger flooded through her. Did he really just proposition her? Clearly her read on men was slipping. It was just her luck that the most gorgeous man she'd laid eyes on in months was also a complete ass.

It took her a moment to recover, and then with a renewed determination for professionalism, she picked up her clipboard and tried to resume the check-in. Anything to get Jason, and everything he suddenly represented, away from her as quickly as possible.

"What room are you in?"

"I thought you weren't interested?" His eyes were hard, but she detected an edge of amusement in his voice. "But if you insist—"

A hot blush shot across her face. "I need it for the form."

"If I knew it, I'd tell you. But I don't have it yet." His grin got wider. "Just put it under Porter."

She scribbled down the name. "And anyone who will be

picking up or dropping Kayden off? I need their names. His mother, perhaps a girlfriend or—"

"My sister's name is Jennifer. I don't have a girlfriend."

Despite how obnoxious he was, the piece of information caused an annoying flutter in her chest. "Okay, and how many days are you staying with us?"

"Five days."

Five days? That was long enough to get to know him. The idea popped into her head before she could stop it. What was she even thinking? He was clearly a player and even if she hadn't sworn off men, Jason should be the last guy she'd consider. She did not need that type of drama in her life.

"Five days is a long time," she said with as much detachment as she could muster. "I'm sure you'll be able to take in a lot of what the Lodge has to offer."

"Doubtful." He rolled his eyes. "I'm here for a family reunion."

"Well, that sounds fun, too." She raised her eyebrows.

"I don't know about that." He shoved his hands in his back pockets, and in an instant, the arrogant man he'd been melted away to reveal the friendly, approachable man she'd met originally. "But it's been awhile since I've been up to the mountains. I forgot how pretty it is up here. I'm looking forward to exploring, maybe a hike or a—"

"Doesn't sound much like a reunion."

"Honestly?" Jason leaned in and whispered. "That was just an excuse to get up to the Lodge."

"Well, now that you're here," Lisa swallowed hard, a chill going down her spine at his closeness, "I hope you find what you're looking for."

He was so close his scent filled her senses. It was a spicy, manly scent, almost like cinnamon, but richer. Almost like chocolate. She fought the urge to pull away even though it was exactly what she should be doing. What was it about this man?

She should have been running in the opposite direction, yet something about him drew her in at the very same time it pushed her away. Confusion roiled through her.

"I'm sure I'll find exactly what I'm looking for," he said after a moment.

His words were loaded with expectation and innuendo. But despite the draw, she had to stay strong and stick to her rules. Especially with a man who so obviously was only in it for the short term. It was probably part of his game to find a holiday fling and she was definitely not in the mood to be anyone's game. No thank you.

Lisa was just about to step back and put a safe distance between them when she heard a voice behind her.

"Lisa?"

She froze and then spun around to see Morgan stood behind her, a frown on her face.

"Is everything okay here?" Morgan asked.

"Of course, I—"

"He was just—"

Morgan looked at both of them in turn. Her eyes narrowed. Eventually she turned to Lisa. "Why don't you take a break?"

Lisa looked back at Jason before she turned to Morgan again. She did not look impressed and no doubt she thought Lisa was hitting on the guests again despite all of Lisa's promises to the contrary. She flicked a look at Jason. Damn him. It was all his fault. He'd done this and he was probably going to go away and have a good laugh with his buddies or his family or whatever, at her expense. She narrowed her eyes and opened her mouth to protest again, but there was no point. Morgan was going to be pissed. That was for sure. Without bothering to look at Jason again, she nodded and walked away.

There was no doubt that Morgan would want to talk about it as soon as she was done with Jason, but she might as well save her breath. Lisa wasn't a fool: despite all of her best efforts since the Gage Mitchell incident, her reputation was a hard one to shake. It's not as if she meant to go over the line—it just happened. Things probably would have been different if her attraction with Gage Mitchell had panned out exactly how she'd planned. But that definitely hadn't worked out, and looking back, it was probably for the best.

No, it was definitely for the best. Lisa smoothed her hair back into a ponytail, and tried to rid herself of the memory. She'd decided then that she really needed to stop acting so loose with men. And she had, too. She spared a quick glance to where Morgan still talked to Jason. For the most part.

"Lisa?" A little voice provided her with the distraction she needed. She looked down at the little girl she'd been painting with earlier.

Lisa crouched so she was at eye level. "What's up, kiddo? Do you need something?"

"Will you play with me? I wanna build blocks, but they keep falling."

Lisa smiled and tucked a strand of Emily's hair behind her ear. "I would love to." She took the little girl by the hand and let her lead the way to the corner where the blocks were kept.

Something caused her to glance in Jason's direction one more time as she handed Emily the first block. He took a piece of paper from Morgan, likely his reminder slip, and turned to leave. But before he did, he looked in her direction and their eyes locked. He opened his mouth as if he wanted to say something, but Lisa shook her head and focused on Emily. Kids were easier.

The second he was out of the Kids Club, Cub Corner or whatever it was called, Jason Porter slammed his hand against the wall and cursed. Seconds later, he looked around to make sure no one had seen him. It was a bad habit, gleaned from too many months up North working in the oil patch, but he knew his twin sister, Jennifer, would rip up one side and down the other if she heard him swear like that.

But sometimes there were no other appropriate words for a situation. Like the way he'd just royally screwed things up with the prettiest girl he'd seen in months. And it wasn't just that she was pretty, although with her blond hair, and womanly curves that just begged for him to—no. He wasn't going to go there. It didn't matter anyway, after the way he'd just behaved. He'd more or less offered her a one-night stand. Regardless whether that was the only type of relationship he cared to have these days, it hadn't been appropriate. And he'd offended her. Any idiot could see that.

But why did it bother him so much? He'd never let it affect him before.

He knew why. Even if he didn't want to admit it. The truth was, Lisa was the first woman he'd been even remotely interested in since Nikki, and that was a long time ago. Not that it mattered, because she wasn't likely to even speak to him again, never mind go out with him. Which was probably a good thing, because dating wasn't an option for him. Not anymore.

He wasn't interested. Not really. At least that's what he could—and probably should—keep telling himself. A date wasn't going to happen, not even if it was just a super casual drink at a hotel where he'd never see the woman again. No. Especially not that. Maybe in a different time, or a different…it didn't matter.

There was no point giving the situation anymore time and energy. Not when he could be out enjoying the mountains or the Lodge itself, which might as well have been the royal palace compared to the basic camps he was used to up North. And he should definitely be enjoying his little nephew, Kayden. It was after all, the only reason he'd agreed to his sister's incessant nagging to go to the stupid family reunion. The last thing he really wanted was to have to make small talk with cousins he hadn't seen since…well, it had been awhile, and he certainly hadn't missed any of them. There was a reason it'd been so long.

But he was here, and he'd play nice, mostly because it would make Jennifer happy and after all, that's what he did. Made his sister happy. He made his way down the corridor to the lobby, where she was hopefully done checking them in. He'd offered to look into the kids club thing for Kayden, mostly to get away from the crush of people, most of whom were relatives who all clambered for a position at the front desk. Details really weren't his thing. He'd let Jen take care of that.

"Hey, buddy." Jason ruffled Kayden's hair and plopped down next to him on one of the plush leather couches in the main reception area. "Where's your mom?"

Kayden pointed to the desk. "She told me to wait here."

"Probably for the best. This is the worst part of staying in a hotel." His nephew nodded his head in agreement. "But do you know what the best part is?"

They looked at each other and said in unison, "The pool!"

"Can we go, Uncle Jason?"

"Of course." He glanced toward his sister who finally, mercifully, made her way toward them. "But let's wait and get settled in our rooms, okay?"

"What are you waiting to do?" Jennifer raised her eyebrow in question. "I'm sure it has something to do with the schedule of events, right?" She smiled and Jason didn't even bother to stifle his groan.

With their dark hair and green eyes, there was no doubt they were siblings, but that's where the similarities ended. Where Jason was always quiet, and preferred to hang out with a few close friends or spend his free time outside, Jennifer had always been the more wild, impulsive twin. She thrived on large groups of people, parties and being the center of attention. A trait that had meant Jason spent most of their high school years playing the role of the protective big brother, making sure the boys who were clamoring for his beautiful sister's attention were worthy. They often weren't. And unfortunately, Jason hadn't been able to prevent his sister from choosing the wrong man to marry and ultimately divorce.

Although, the one good thing that came from that union was his nephew. And that was a pretty damn good thing. Plus, now that she was a mother, Jennifer had completely changed, except when it came to wanting be around lots of people. Hence, the reunion.

"Come on, Jason." She shoved an envelope at him. "That's why we're here."

"What's this?" He eyed the envelope somewhat suspiciously but didn't open it.

"Your itinerary for the weekend."

With one last look at the envelope, Jason stood and shoved it in his back pocket. "Right." He grabbed the bags. "Why don't we go find our rooms?"

Kayden leapt up and led the way across the large timber framed lobby to the bank of elevators. Jason smiled and gathered up the bags. As they made their way across the room, Jason was careful not to make eye contact with any of his cousins. He knew he couldn't avoid talking to them forever, but he did plan to put it off for as long as possible. Instead he focused on the large picture windows that covered the entire back wall of the lobby, and the magnificent view they afforded. It had been a long time since he'd been in the mountains, too long, and he couldn't wait to get out there.

"You know you're going to have to hang out with them a

little bit." Jennifer read his mind, the way she always did, but Jason only shrugged and shook his head.

"Not if I can help it."

"Jason." She turned to look at him as they waited for the elevator. "That's why you're here. It's a family reunion."

"No." He stabbed his finger at the button again. "That's why you're here. I'm here to be with you. And Kayden." He smiled at his nephew. "And that's exactly what I plan on doing. And you know, I checked out that kids club thing." The face of the beautiful blond, with her fiery eyes glaring at him, flashed through his mind. "But I don't know if that's the right thing for Kayden."

"Why not? The lady at the desk said they did lots of fun things, like crafts and hikes and even scavenger hunts."

"Scavenger hunts?" Kayden was always listening, and had twigged onto the one thing that he'd liked the sound of. "I wanna do that."

"I'm sure we can sign you up—"

"I don't think it's—"

Kayden looked between them and shook his head. He was used to his mom and his uncle disagreeing. He also knew his mom made the final decision.

"We'll sign you up." She shot Jason a look.

"He already is," Jason mumbled and thankfully, the elevator arrived and without another word, he picked up the bags. "The day after tomorrow." There was no point arguing with his sister. She'd win. She always did. Besides, Jennifer was right: Kayden would have fun in the kids group, and there weren't very many little cousins his age. The whole family reunion would be even more excruciatingly boring for his nephew than it would be for him.

And more than boring, and dealing with his extended family, it would be the constant reminder of what Jason had once, and had lost.

Their rooms were next to each other, down a long hall, and after Jason dropped the bags in Jennifer and Kayden's room, he looked forward to a bit of time alone. Of course, his sister had other plans. Before he even had time to cross the room and open the curtains, there was a knock on the door that attached their two rooms. He could ignore it. Pretend he hadn't heard it. But that would only buy him a few minutes. When his sister wanted something, there was no way she gave up.

With a flick, he unlatched the deadbolt and seconds later, the door opened, and his sister stepped inside. "Kayden's jumping on the beds, trying to decide which one he wants to sleep in, so I thought I'd come and see how you're doing."

"Why wouldn't I be doing okay?" Jason tugged the cord that opened the thick curtains and let the sunlight spill into the room. It was a beautiful fall day, and although he knew the weather could change in an instant up in the mountains, for the moment it was beautiful.

"Come on, Jason. I know you. I know this can't be easy."

Without turning away from the view, he said, "What? Being around all these people who share our name, but not our lives? Who pretend to care about us, but really just want a good story to talk about around their dinner table at Sunday night dinner? You think that's hard? I don't understand."

"That's not fair." He turned to see his twin, with her arms crossed over her chest. "You know that's not fair. They're not all like that."

"But most are."

Jennifer started to shake her head in protest, but turned it into a shrug instead. "Okay, I admit, our family wasn't totally supportive after…well, when Nikki died, I know they weren't the best." The mention of her name prompted the familiar pain in his chest, although admittedly, it wasn't as sharp as it had been.

"No, Jen. Our *family*. Mom, Dad, you and Kayden. You guys were great. Everyone else, well they can go to—"

"Uncle Jason!" Kayden's head appeared in the doorway, promoting a warning look from Jennifer. Not that he needed it —Jason would never swear in front of his nephew. Not intentionally anyway. "Isn't it cool? Our rooms are totally attached."

Jason grinned. How could he not? His real family was right here in the room with him. With the exception of his parents, who had to take a last-minute business trip instead of joining them. It was probably for the best anyway, considering his dad mostly shared Jason's feelings regarding his own family, despite the fact that most of them worked for the family business, Porter Properties. Jason had somehow managed to avoid taking a position there, despite his father's constant asking. Nikki's death had changed a lot of things. Too many.

Chapter Two

"YOU KNOW WE NEED TO TALK." For a moment, Lisa pretended she hadn't heard Morgan, and continued to pack up her purse. "Come to the Grill with me and we'll make it less formal. But we still need to discuss it," Morgan insisted. "It's my job to review a situation like this. Besides, it's time for a performance review."

Lisa sighed and zipped up her purse. She knew it was coming. Not only was it time for her quarterly review, but after what happened with that arrogant, player of a guest, she'd known a chat with her boss was imminent. "It doesn't seem like I have much of a choice." She turned around and swung her bag over her shoulder.

Morgan smiled. "You don't really. But I'm your friend, too. So we might as well have a drink while we chat. Right?"

Lisa couldn't help but return her friend's smile. Even though she knew she'd be chastised for something that was totally not her fault, she also knew Morgan would be fair about it.

"Let's go." Lisa shook her head and held the door open.

As they walked down through the expansive halls of the

Lodge, Lisa looked around and tried to remember why she'd come to Castle Mountain in the first place. She'd been there over a year, ever since she'd decided she couldn't stay in her small town for one more second. Originally she'd been looking for a summer job, something to get her away from the reputation she'd managed to create for herself back home. But it didn't take long for her to fall in love with the Lodge, and the friendships she'd made. The only issue was that she'd inadvertently caused herself the same problem with men in a whole new place. At least, she had. But all of that was going to change. It had changed. At least until Jason had walked in. Lisa's mind drifted back to the man with his ridiculously large arms. Arms that could—

"Hey." Morgan snapped her fingers in front of Lisa's face. "Are you listening to me?"

"Of course." Morgan frowned, so Lisa shook her head and apologized. "Sorry, I was just thinking about something. What did you say?"

Morgan shot her a look, but didn't press the issue. "Let's find a table first."

They scanned the room, which was already filling up. The Grill was a favorite of both staff and guests and it wasn't unusual that it was busy, but Lisa had hoped it might be a quiet night. No such luck, but they did have a bit of luck finding a table and soon they were seated across from each other at a high table in the middle of the room.

As soon as they were settled, Lisa focused on her friend. "What were you saying earlier?"

"I asked you what you thought about taking the kids on a hike soon."

"I think it's a great idea," she said. "I love hiking and the weather's supposed to be nice for the next few days. We might as well take advantage of it."

The weather in the mountains in November was unpredictable. They could easily get an early storm that would dump enough snow that would stay all winter, or they could have an extended autumn and enjoy milder temperatures the way they had been.

"That's exactly what I was thinking," Morgan said. She grabbed the menu card off the table. "It's going to be a long winter; it always is. So we might as well get outside while we can. And Bo said the trails were still good when he was up there a few days ago. It should be fun."

They each ordered a spicy Caesar, a Lodge specialty drink, and a plate of the Grill's famous nachos to nibble on. It wasn't until their drinks were in front of them that Morgan got down to business and the real reason they were there.

"You know we need to talk about what happened today," Morgan said. "So, go ahead and tell me why you would hit on a guest after everything that happened."

Lisa sighed and swirled the celery stick around in her drink before she pulled it out and took a bite. She didn't respond to her friend, but raised her eyebrows instead.

"It's not the first time I've gotten a complaint about your flirting, Lisa."

Lisa swallowed hard and almost choked on the celery. "He complained?"

"No." Morgan shook her head. "He didn't and to be fair, I haven't had a complaint about it in months. But he might have if I hadn't stepped in. What was that all about, anyway?"

Of course Morgan hadn't received any complaints about her behavior. Lisa fought the urge to fire back at her friend, but it wasn't her fault; Lisa only had herself to blame for her past behavior. But things were different now, and there hadn't been any complaints because she was behaving herself. She hadn't so much as winked at a man in months and that included other staff members. For all intents and purposes, Lisa had been living like a nun and to get strung up because of Jason's behavior...well, that wasn't going to happen.

She took a deep breath and in an effort to calm down, Lisa turned her attention to her drink and dipped the celery stick in again, before she abandoned it for the straw. There was no point answering Morgan. They both knew there wasn't going to be an answer that would satisfy either of them. Even if Lisa denied what Morgan thought she saw, she wasn't naive enough to believe that it would be enough. Friends or not, Morgan took her role very seriously, and she wouldn't stand for any misbehavior from her staff. Not anymore.

"You need to talk to me."

Lisa took a long sip and let the spicy drink fill her senses.

"Lisa."

"Okay." Lisa pushed her drink away and stared at Morgan. "But I don't know what you want me to say. The truth is, he flirted with me. He more or less propositioned me, and I turned him down; he was insulted and got a bit of an attitude. End of story."

Morgan narrowed her eyes and waited. And waited.

"Honestly," Lisa said. "It wasn't anything. And it definitely wasn't me. I told you, I've changed. I'm totally sworn off men. I don't want anything to do with them."

Morgan tilted her head.

"I don't," Lisa insisted. She pulled her drink toward her and took another long sip. At the rate she was going, she'd need a refill in no time.

"I know the whole Gage Mitchell thing—"

"That wasn't a thing. His PR rep hated me and made it seem way worse than it was." Lisa focused on her drink. She did not want to relive that situation. Gage was a huge celebrity who had stayed at the Lodge to escape from his life for a little bit. Of course Lisa had come on to him; he was gorgeous. Anybody would have. And he'd been interested in her, too. At least until that meddling PR rep got involved. And she may have tried to insinuate something had happened, but that was all in the past. "That's ancient history. I'm over it and I'm totally over men. I told you."

"I know. I know. But, all men?" Morgan's voice was serious. Lisa didn't meet her gaze because she knew it'd be full of concern, and worse, pity. "I'm actually a little worried about you. I agree that you shouldn't be dating the guests, but what about some of the other guys? It's not like you. And there are plenty of men here, you just have to...well, will you let me set you up?"

Thankfully, Lisa was saved from answering by the arrival of a large platter of nachos the waitress put between them. She immediately pulled a chip from the pile and stuffed it in her mouth. The last thing she wanted was for Morgan to set her up. Well, maybe it wasn't the last thing. She did miss going on dates and the companionship of a man. Morgan was right; it wasn't like her to be single for so long. But maybe that wasn't a bad thing.

"I'm not leaving here until you talk to me about this," Morgan said. "You're my friend and I care about you." She picked up a chip of her own. "And besides that, I really don't want to have to write you up for inappropriate behavior with guests. Don't put me in that position, okay?"

Lisa nodded, instantly guilty and defensive. "I'm not trying to make things hard on you, Morgan. I'm not. I told you, what happened today had nothing to do with me." She grabbed a napkin and twisted it in her hands. "And sometimes I forget that you're my boss, but I promise, I'm not going to screw this up. I love my job and the Lodge. I won't mess with it, not for anything." *Or anyone*, she echoed in her head.

"You're beautiful and smart and so great with kids. You're so much more than all that."

"I know." She said the words, but her thoughts turned to

Jason, who'd given her an unbelievably sexy smile while he was busy being an ass. Just thinking of the earlier incident aggravated her. Something about him got under her skin. And she hated it when men did that to her. Especially when she was sworn off them.

Morgan picked at the pile of cheesy chips in front of her and pulled one free from the stack. "I'm not going to get all therapist with you, but—"

"Good."

Morgan frowned at her. "But," she said with emphasis. "There has to be a reason you shy away from relationships." She popped the chip into her mouth and chewed thoughtfully for a moment. "What was your mom and dad's relationship like?"

Lisa froze, her drink halfway to her mouth. Morgan had hit close to home. A little too close. She swallowed hard and took a sip of her drink. "It was fine," she lied. "So your amateur therapy skills are seriously flawed."

She stuffed another nacho chip in her mouth to keep from saying more. Her parents' relationship had been far from fine. In fact, Lisa hadn't seen her dad since she was six and he told her he was going to the store. He never came back. She wasn't about to tell Morgan that, though. Even if she was the closest friend Lisa had. There was no doubt Morgan would come up with all kinds of theories surrounding Lisa's absentee father and her intense need for male attention. And the worst part was, she wouldn't be far off.

"Look," Lisa said after a moment. "Things have been better lately, right? I mean, there haven't been any complaints. Including today," she added pointedly. "So, let's not mess with it. No setups. Just let things be. Deal?"

Morgan examined her for a moment before nodding. "It's a deal. Because honestly, I don't want anything to affect your job.

You're too good—I can't lose you because of a silly reputation."

A reputation. She hated that word. But that's what it was. For better or worse. "Okay, good. No men."

"At least for a few weeks." Morgan smiled. "And in the meantime, I'll talk to Bo, and we'll see if we can set you up on a real date in a few weeks."

Lisa groaned and rolled her eyes. So much for no setups. Bo was the outdoor activities director at the Lodge, who also happened to be the love of Morgan's life. Despite all her friend's protesting about Lisa's flirting, they both knew she wanted to see Lisa happily settled the way she was.

"I told you—"

"Well, you don't have a choice, because I'm going to make it happen." Morgan flashed her a brilliant smile, and Lisa shook her head with a smile of her own. "And guess what? I just spoke with Andi the other day and she's going to bring the baby up to the Lodge for a visit. She wasn't sure if Colin could make it or not, but it will be good to see her and meet the baby finally."

Andi and Colin were well loved around the Lodge. They'd fallen in love there during a Christmas storm, and their relationship had become a bit of a legend among the guests. Especially after their wedding the following year. And now with a baby, Andi and Colin had the love story everyone wanted. Everyone, including Lisa. Even if she didn't admit it.

"That reminds me," Morgan changed tracks again. "I need to call Bo. I'll be back in a second, okay?"

Lisa nodded and Morgan slipped out of her chair. "I'll be here." As Morgan walked away, she mumbled under her breath, "Not flirting with anyone."

She picked up another chip but discarded it back on the pile and sat up to scan the room for the first time. The Grill usually held a mixture of guests and off-shift employees, and tonight was no different. There were the usual clusters of Lodge staff members, who were likely out for a good time. They wanted to drink too much, play some pool and do a whole lot of flirting with whoever was around. That was the group Lisa usually hung out with. She raised her drink in a wave when a few of them looked in her direction. But she turned away before she could make eye contact with anyone. She was serious when she'd told Morgan she'd changed.

Lisa was sick of her *reputation,* and she wanted nothing more than to be rid of it. There was a reason she flirted with guys so much: if she were honest, she loved the attention. But it wasn't enough anymore. It hadn't been for a while. What she really wanted was someone who'd think the world of her. Someone who cared about her, and asked her about her dreams and goals. She wanted someone who loved her and wanted to be with her. Which was the other reason she'd decided to turn her life around. Not only did she want to protect her job, but she also knew she wouldn't get what she wanted, doing what she was doing.

And even if she wasn't ready to admit it to her friend, Lisa wanted a relationship. A real one. And despite the fact that she absolutely loved the Lodge, recently her thoughts had turned to leaving. Maybe it was the only way to get what she really wanted?

It was too much to think about. She sighed and drained the last of her drink. The way the night was going, she was definitely going to need another. She took a quick look around, and not seeing the waitress, decided to head straight to the bar.

It was a busy night in the Grill, and Lisa had to squeeze her way through a bit of a crowd to get to the front of the bar. She angled her shoulders and pushed her way through a small gap, but her foot caught on a stool and she stumbled, falling into the man who stood next to her.

"Oh." She caught herself and twisted to face forward.

"Are you—"

She turned so she faced the man, and looked directly in Jason's eyes. His words died on his lips as they turned into a smile.

"Well, hello again."

His eyes were the brightest shade of green she'd ever seen. For a moment, she was at a loss for words. He was the last person she thought she'd run into. And definitely the worst at that moment.

Lisa swallowed hard. "I'm sorry. I tripped a little. I didn't mean to push you."

Jason smiled, and she couldn't help but notice a little dimple she hadn't seen earlier. "It's fine," he said. "I can hold my own."

"I'm sure you…I didn't mean to…" Lisa squeezed her eyes shut for a second and tried to pull herself together. When she opened them again, he smiled at her. Borderline laughed at her, in fact. "Well, I'm sorry I pushed," she said finally. Aware that he watched her, she turned away and tried to get the bartender's attention.

"Let me buy you a drink."

What? It was only a few hours ago he'd been making a point that he wasn't interested in her. A very solid point. Or was he interested? He'd thrown so many mixed messages at her, she didn't even know anymore. Lisa turned slowly and narrowed her eyes. "I'm good, thanks." She looked away again and raised her arm at Dan, who tended bar. He saw her, smiled and made his way toward her.

"Hey, Lisa. What can I get you?"

"A spicy Caesar." She returned his smile. "And probably one for Morgan, too."

"Done."

Dan turned his back to make the drinks and Lisa reached

for her purse, which was always slung across her body. It wasn't.

"Dammit." She looked around as she tried to remember whether she'd grabbed it from the Cub Club before she'd left. She hadn't.

"Don't worry," Jason said. "I've got it."

Lisa didn't know whether she was more annoyed that he'd read the situation so perfectly, or that he was trying to be nice.

"You don't have—"

"I got it," Jason said again. He handed Dan his credit card as the bartender returned with the finished drinks. Dan raised an eyebrow in Lisa's direction and turned away.

Lisa could only shake her head and mumble a thank-you. No doubt by the time she got back to the staff apartments later, there'd be some story about her and Jason.

"That's it?"

"I said thank you," Lisa repeated. "I told you it wasn't necessary. Dan could have put them on my tab." She picked up the glasses. Needing some space between them, she tried to push her way through the crowd that had only grown larger while she'd been standing there. "I should be getting back."

"Hey." Jason grabbed her arm. "I wanted to apologize for earlier."

Lisa froze.

"I didn't mean for there to be any kind of misunderstanding or bad feelings between us."

Lisa turned and looked at him again. He really was good-looking, more than good-looking. But she wasn't going to let that cloud her mind. "There's nothing between us." She lied, because the way her body reacted to his touch, there was definitely something between them.

"You're beautiful," he continued, and she melted a little bit. "But I didn't—"

She jerked her arm away. There it was: the but. And she

wasn't going to stick around and listen to it again. He'd done enough damage for one day. "It's fine," she said. "I'm not interested, remember?" The lies came fast, but they didn't come easy and if she hung around too much longer, she might be tempted into telling the truth. That she really was interested in him, or at least she might be if things were different, much different. She took one more look at him and the dimple she desperately wanted to touch. Lisa exhaled hard. "Excuse me." And before he could say another word, she ducked away, found a gap in the crowd, and made her escape.

Jason watched her walk across the room, back to her table, and for at least the dozenth time that day, he wished he hadn't been such an ass to her earlier. Something about her was different. Sure, she was clearly beautiful and probably had no problem getting the attention of any man in the place. Hell, probably anywhere. But there was something else, too. Something he was positive all those men who gave her attention didn't see. But he saw it; he just couldn't quite put his finger on it. Not yet.

An unfamiliar twinge, deep in his gut, pulled him toward Lisa. He hadn't been so interested in a woman for a very long. Not since he first met Nikki. And even then, it wasn't the same. His feet moved in Lisa's direction, his eyes not leaving her. It was ridiculous, and she clearly didn't want to talk to him—not that he could blame her—but he needed to apologize. Make her accept his apology. Even if he didn't understand why.

"Jason."

He froze at the familiar voice. It had been years, exactly four. But he'd been expecting it. Jason turned slowly, not bothering to hide his disdain. "Cousin. It's been a long time."

Conrad Porter, his first cousin on his father's side, three years his senior, stood in front of him, and looked every bit the smug, know-it-all Jason remembered him to be. "Well, if you bothered to come to any of our family functions instead of hiding up North in that...camp, you wouldn't be such a stranger."

Jason swallowed the bile that rose in his throat. "Well, cousin. Some of us have to work for a living." Conrad and his younger brother, Chase, had both worked in the family business since high school graduation, if you called golfing all day and wining and dining clients working. Neither of them were strangers to the soft life, and for whatever reason, they couldn't seem to understand why Jason wanted nothing to do with it. He preferred to work for a living, and pave his own way. Sure, there'd been talks about Jason going to work for the property management firm, and he hadn't totally ruled it out. Nothing would make his father happier. But if and when he decided to trade it all in for the corporate life, he'd do it on his own terms. Terms that included legitimately working hard.

Conrad slapped him on the back and left his arm draped around Jason's shoulders. Jason had to swallow his disgust. It wasn't just his lazy ways that caused the animosity between them. The bad blood between them ran far deeper than that.

"Don't be that way, Cuz." Conrad turned Jason and smoothly led him toward a table filled with his relatives. "One day we'll convince you to join our ranks, and then you'll see just how much work it really is."

He doubted it but there was no point saying so.

"Come have a drink and let's catch up."

He sighed, and accepted the situation. After all, he was at a family reunion. He should probably make some attempt to actually reunite with his family. His smile was forced, but he doubted very much that anyone would notice they were too caught up in the details of their own lives. With a shake of his head, he resigned himself to at least an hour of small talk before he could get away, and nodded his greeting to the various people.

Jason strategically chose a seat near his first cousin, Emily. She'd always been one of his favorite cousins. "Nice to see you, Em." He dropped a kiss on her cheek and once he was settled in his seat, tried to peek and see whether he could see Lisa. Too many people stood between him and her table, so reluctantly, he turned his attention to the conversation.

"We're glad you came," Emily said. "It's been too long."

"Some would say not long enough," Jason said, and when Emily frowned, he immediately felt bad. "How have you been? Keeping busy?"

She nodded, her kind smile returning. "I'm trying."

"Where's that husband of yours?" Jason had always liked Emily's husband, Nolan.

"He was pulled into a game of darts."" She pointed in his direction and as if he could sense her, Nolan turned and waved. Emily smiled before she turned her attention back to Jason. She put her hand on Jason's arm and squeezed. "We do miss you. I know it's been hard since—"

"It's been fine."

"Jason."

He shook his head. "I don't want to talk about it." And he didn't. The last time he'd seen most of the people in the room was at Nikki's funeral. And he knew they meant well, but they also didn't know the whole truth. As if a hit-and-run killing his fiancée wasn't bad enough, he'd had to deal with the truth of where she'd been that night and with whom. His entire life had imploded that night, and learning the truth once and for all about the woman he'd thought he'd loved, and the man he'd considered one of his closest friends, sent him into a dark spiral.

He'd protected his family from the worst of it; after all, that's what family did. If they knew the truth—that it was their golden boy, Conrad's house, Nikki had been coming back from that night—it would have fractured the entire family. Even in his grief, Jason wouldn't do that. But he also couldn't stick around and watch everyone behave as if his life hadn't been torn apart. And when he left, he'd sworn never again would he put himself and his heart out there the way he had for Nikki.

"Honestly," he said to Emily after a moment. "I just want to get through this little trip." He forced a smile. "Now tell me what's new with you? Don't tell me they've actually brainwashed you into liking things at Porter Properties?"

"It's not that bad." She tucked a strand of hair behind her ear and twirled her straw. "You know there's a spot for you? We all want you there, Jason. We need your management skills. Please tell me you'll consider it?"

He took a long pull on his beer before he answered her. The truth was, he had considered it. After Nikki died, all he'd wanted was to get as far away from his family and his life as possible. He'd done that. Managing a crew on an oil rig in Northern Canada had accomplished that perfectly. But his dad was getting older and he wanted to retire. He'd pressured Jason to come on board with Porter Properties before it was too late and his cousins weaseled their way into the top management positions. His father and his uncle had worked too hard building up a business to have it turned over to Conrad, who would no doubt run it into the ground. Besides, he was getting a little stir crazy with Northern living. Maybe it was time for a change. Maybe it was time to go home.

"You never know, Em. I might actually consider it one of these days."

Her smile lit up her face. She squealed and called over to her brothers. "You'll never guess—"

"Whoa." Jason silenced her. "Let me think about it a bit more before you go announcing anything to anyone, okay?"

Emily nodded, but she didn't bother hiding her smile.

"Okay, but I think it's great. You know I love the family business, but..."

"But?"

"I think it might be time for me to take a break." She patted her stomach. "At least by summer."

It took Jason a minute to figure out what his cousin was getting at, but as soon as she rolled her eyes and held her arms out in front of her, he got it. With a whoop, Jason jumped out of his seat and pulled his cousin into his arms for a big hug. The familiar twinge of regret was there, too. But it was overshadowed by his genuine happiness for Emily. The pain that he'd lost his opportunity for a family when he lost Nikki was always present, but over time it faded, just the way his hurt did.

"That's great news." His smile was genuine. "Let me buy you a drink. A ginger ale, of course."

"Of course."

To Jason's surprise, the next hour flew by and he got swept up in Emily's plans, and he found that he enjoyed some of the conversation with people he hadn't seen in years. It wasn't nearly as painful as he'd thought it would be. Especially because he kept an eye on Lisa the entire evening. She was beautiful and if he wasn't sure that he'd be shot down again, he'd happily go talk to her again. But he wasn't a fool and only a fool would keep going back for more when it was perfectly clear that she had no interest in him.

Not that he could blame her. He'd done it to himself. He hadn't exactly been warm and fuzzy, and for the life of him he couldn't figure out why he'd been such a jerk. Of course she wasn't going to be interested in him when he'd treated her like a booty call. But it was probably for the best, anyway. He wasn't interested. At least he shouldn't be.

"Why don't you go talk to her?"

Before he could even realize he'd been caught out, Jason shook his head. "Nah. I'm not going there."

"Why not? It's been four years. It's okay to move on."

"You sound like my sister."

"Family resemblance and all that." She smirked and tilted her head in a way that was very much like Jennifer. "Besides, you know we're right."

"No." He shook his head and stood up. "I should go. It's getting late."

"Jason."

He threw some money on the table, more than enough to cover his drinks. "It's not going to happen, Emily. I'll see you tomorrow, okay?"

He walked away before she could pry further or ask him why it wasn't going to happen. Because he honestly didn't know whether it was because of him vowing to never have anything more serious than a fling, or Lisa not wanting anything to do with him. It was a question that bothered him more than he cared to admit because never before had it come up.

Chapter Three

"WHAT DO you think about going for a swim today?" Lisa tried to ignore her friend, Astrid's, voice calling to her, breaking through her dreams, interrupting her long overdue sleep-in. She tugged the pillow over her head and buried deeper under her quilt but she knew it wasn't a long-term solution. Not where Astrid was involved.

"I know you're not really sleeping." Astrid's singsong voice was closer. Too close. "The vibe is all wrong in here and I can practically feel your energy aura from here." Before Lisa could stop it, the covers flipped back and she stared, bleary eyed, up at her friend. Although, if she didn't back away quickly and let her sleep, she couldn't be sure she'd be her friend for long.

"Go away."

"I don't think so. Sleeping in so long isn't good for the spirit and your spirit needs all the work it can get."

Lisa ignored the quip and rolled over on her side. "Eight in the morning is hardly sleeping in for too long." She groaned. "Besides, weren't you out at some sort of party last night? You should be the one sleeping in."

When Morgan decided to move in with Bo, she'd insisted

that Astrid was a fabulous roommate and although the two women had grown close, the jury was still out on whether she was a fabulous roommate or not. Usually her crystals, incense, and random comments about her aura energy flow, or whatever it was, didn't bother Lisa. At least not too much. But at eight in the morning on a rare day off, anything would bother her.

"No way. It's bad karma to sleep in on such a nice day. Before you know it the snow will be here, and our chance will be gone."

Lisa cracked one eye open a slit. "Our chance to swim in the pool? I hardly think that chance will go away."

Astrid waved her hands in a bizarre pantomime motion that probably had something to do with evoking some type of positive energy that Lisa must certainly be lacking, and let out an exasperated sigh. "No. The chance to absorb the power from the day. It's not all that usual to have such nice weather in November. I can't remember the last time we went this long without our first snowfall. It's a good sign. A sign that the universes are—"

"Okay." Lisa gave in. Anything to get her to stop talking about universes, power and the energy of the earth or whatever she was going to go on about next. "I'll go swimming with you. But don't think I'm happy about it. And next time you have a day off, I'm going to..."

There was no point finishing the thought. If Astrid ever did have a day off, the last thing she'd be worried about would be sleeping in. With a sigh, Lisa resigned herself to the fact that whether she liked it or not, she'd be starting her day. She might as well make the best of it.

"Give me five minutes." She rubbed her eyes and swung her legs out of bed. "And a coffee. I'm not doing anything without caffeine."

. . .

Twenty minutes later, the friends were on the wooded path and made their way through the thick pines, toward the main lodge and the pool area. As employees, they didn't have free access to the pool facilities, but they had a punch pass for some access and were encouraged not to use it during peak times. Most of the staff didn't bother, but Lisa loved nothing more than a long soak in the outside hot tub, surrounded by the mountains with the smell of pine floating on the breeze. It was her idea of a heaven, which was why she hadn't protested harder.

Fortunately the pool area wasn't very busy in the morning. Only a few people were in the pool, and even fewer in the hot tub.

"Come on," Astrid called. After she threw her towel on a nearby chair, she headed to the deep end of the pool. "Come do some laps with me."

"No way."

"It's good exercise." Astrid pulled her long skinny braids back into a ponytail. "Water helps align your chakras."

"My chakras are fine."

"They're really not." Astrid put her hand on her hip and opened her mouth to say something else, likely to tell Lisa how she needed to work on an aura adjustment or do a smudge or some such thing.

"I'll be in the hot tub, soaking, because that's good for my chakras, my muscles, and pretty much everything else I can think of."

Astrid waved her away. Lisa waited a beat and watched her friend enter the deep end of the pool with a graceful dive before she turned and made her way across the tile and into the hot tub. With each step into the hot water, she could feel herself relax. The water was magical.

Lisa avoided making eye contact with any of the guests, especially the male ones. It was just easier that way.

The pool was half inside and half outside, and that's

exactly where Lisa headed. She pushed through the strips of vinyl that separated the two spaces and was rewarded with the warm autumn sunshine on her face. She located an empty spot away from everyone else, and sank down onto the bench so her shoulders were completely covered by the water. A sigh escaped her lips as she lifted her face up and took in the cloudless blue sky.

She could sit like that all day and maybe she might. Laundry, groceries, and all the other details that she needed to take care of could wait. Nothing was more important than soaking. Besides, didn't Astrid say something about it being good for her aura or something? That was important. She should probably listen to her friend. Her eyes drifted shut.

She might have dozed off, but a shriek followed by a splash and a large wave that doused Lisa's face effectively broke the magic spell of her serene moment. Her eyes popped open. She sat up with a start and looked for the source of the splash.

A little boy, a grin on his face, splashed a few feet away. He was cute, and so pleased with himself, any irritation she felt with being interrupted vanished. She shook her head slightly and smiled. He could obviously swim, but Lisa couldn't see an adult who clearly belonged to him, and her childcare instincts kicked in.

"Hey." She got the little boy's attention. "Where's your mom and dad?"

The boy shrugged.

"Are you here by yourself?" The pool area didn't have a lifeguard on duty because there was a rule about children under the age of twelve being accompanied by an adult. What type of parent would let a little boy swim in the pool by himself? "Well, maybe we should go find your parents. What's your name?"

"Kayden."

The name sounded familiar, but Lisa saw so many kids at

the Cub Club, it was likely she'd had another child with the same name, because she didn't recognize the cutie in front of her. "It's nice to meet you, Kayden. Should we go find who you belong to?"

"That would be me."

The deep voice behind her sent chills up her spine, and caused something in her core to tighten in reflex. Lisa turned slowly. *There's no way. It couldn't be—*

"Uncle Jason."

Uncle Jason?

Of course.

What was it about the guy? He just kept popping up. She couldn't catch a break. The sight of him shirtless, water dripping off his six-pack, a sexy smile at work on his face, was nothing short of torture, because nothing was ever going to happen with him.

"Well, I'm glad Kayden has supervision of some kind." She turned away. Satisfied that the boy wasn't in any immediate danger, she could go back to her soaking and relaxing. And that's just what she intended to do.

"It's nice to see you again."

She stopped. His words washed over her. She should just continue walking and pretend she hadn't heard him. She should go back to her spot where she could continue enjoying the hot pool and the day. But there was something in his voice. She couldn't help it. Lisa turned and looked at him, careful to keep her eyes on his face and away from the very hard body that her fingers instinctively wanted to touch.

"It does seem that you're everywhere I seem to be."

"Or maybe it's the other way around." His eyes flashed with the tease.

Determined not to let him affect her, she shrugged as casually as she could. "The Lodge isn't really all that big when you're trying to avoid someone."

The dangerous smile on his face vanished and Lisa instantly regretted her words, mostly because she wasn't trying to avoid him. Not really. But before she could think of anything else to say, Kayden was there and splashed water up at his uncle.

"Uncle Jason. Let's go. You said we could go to the cold pool."

His eyes never leaving hers, he nodded. "Absolutely, buddy, because you're not really supposed to be jumping in the hot tub. You should apologize to Lisa for disturbing her."

"It's okay." Lisa turned her attention away from Jason, to the much safer male. "I think I'm going to see you tomorrow anyway. Are you ready for a hike?"

Kayden nodded eagerly before he took off for the pool. Lisa didn't bother to see whether Jason would say anything else to her. She wasn't going to risk everything for a fling. Not even one with a man like Jason. And he'd made it perfectly clear that's all he wanted. She wasn't that kind of girl. Not anymore. But something intrigued her about him. Which meant it was probably for the best that after a second, Jason followed his nephew's lead, and with only a quick glance back to her, took off across the large hot pool. Yes, it was definitely for the best, she decided as she settled herself back into the water. All she had to do was mind her own business. She should have known that would be easier said than done. She'd only had her eyes closed for a moment before a voice interrupted her silence.

"The view out here is incredible."

Lisa waited for a moment before she opened her eyes to see the source of the voice. The pools were never so busy in the morning: what were the odds that the day she wanted to be there, they were overrun with guests? Slowly, she opened her eyes to see a man sat next to her, a smile on his face. Only a few days ago, Lisa would have found him extremely attractive, but compared to Jason, the man in front of her wasn't nearly as good-looking. Something about him and the way he looked at her rubbed her the wrong way. But he was a guest.

"It is amazing out here, isn't it?" She answered him and angled away from him slightly.

"It is." The man slid closer. "But I wasn't talking about the mountains." His grin was wicked, and slightly familiar. "The name's Conrad."

Anger flared through him, and Jason had to force himself to look away from the scene he'd watched through the large picture window that looked out to the hot tub. The urge to hold his cousin's overgrown head under the water until he begged for mercy was overwhelming. It was also irrational, particularly because Lisa wasn't his. He had no claim over her, and she'd made it clear that she wasn't interested in what he was offering. Hell, he didn't even know what he was offering. It was only because of reflex that he'd tried to suggest a one-night stand. He hadn't meant it. Not really. She wasn't even his type, because he no longer had a type. And now she would barely give him the time of day. Which was fine by him.

Except it wasn't really. Despite everything in his head that told him he had no business pursuing anything with her, not even a casual conversation, he couldn't help the draw he felt toward her. He'd never felt that before. Even with Nikki, things had been different. Their attraction had been more of a slow build until they settled into a comfortable companionship. At least he thought they had. As it turned out, there a was a lot—

"Uncle Jason! Watch me."

With a small snort in Conrad and Lisa's direction, Jason did just that, and turned to watch Kayden cannonball into the pool. The kid had no fear for such a little guy, and he never failed to make Jason smile. He was a good kid, and the closeness they shared was even more special considering Jason would never have kids of his own. That required a partner.

Kayden's head popped out of the water and Jason reached out to pull him over. "That's awesome, buddy. Where did you learn how to do that?"

"Swim lessons."

"They taught you how to cannonball in swim lessons?" He raised an eyebrow at his nephew, who only smiled in response.

"Yup, and they taught me to do this, too." Before Jason could back away from what he knew was coming, a splash of water hit him smack in the face and with a shriek, Kayden took off and swam as fast as he could to the other end of the pool.

"What kind of swim lessons does your mother have you in?" He laughed and waited another beat before he dove under the water and quickly caught up to Kayden. With ease, Jason flipped him up in the air and caught him again with a splash.

"Again!"

Like the good uncle he was, Jason obliged and spent the next few minutes tossing Kayden into the air, occasionally letting him go under before pulling him to the surface. With every spurt and sputter of water, Kayden's smile only got bigger. But soon, despite the happiness written on his face, exhaustion was also there.

"What do you say we go hang out in the room now?" And before Kayden could protest, he added, "I think they have room service and I bet if your mom's not looking, we can order milkshakes."

Not about to turn down the offer of illicit milkshakes, Kayden quickly agreed. With a laugh, Jason wiped the water from his face, and slicked back his hair as he turned around.

His smile froze on his face when he saw Lisa. He'd managed to forget about her and his sleazy cousin while he played with Kayden, but to his annoyance, the sight of her instantly made his heart race. He glanced around but Conrad was nowhere to be seen.

He knew he shouldn't bother with her. He knew he should just leave her to Conrad, because after all, isn't that how it would end up anyway? But he couldn't stop himself when his body moved in her direction. She was still in the hot tub, this time inside, her head tilted back; she was obviously relaxed and enjoying her soak. It wouldn't be nice to interrupt her. And besides, what would it achieve? Nothing. He knew that. Yet, it didn't seem to matter.

"Kayden," Jason called.

"Right here."

He looked down to see the little boy smiled up at him. "Right. I think we should probably go have a soak in the hot tub before we get changed. It's good for your muscles to soak after a workout."

"Was that a workout?"

Jason bent down and hoisted Kayden up so he could carry him on his back. "Absolutely. Now let me see you flex."

With his mouth set in a determined line, Kayden lifted his arm up and squeezed as tightly as he could. Jason made sure to swallow his smile when he saw how serious his nephew was.

"That's a huge muscle, Kay. You're getting so strong."

"Not as strong as you." Kayden's face fell, and Jason tilted it back up. He stared into the boy's eyes.

"Not yet, buddy. But soon."

"Let me see your muscle, Uncle Jason."

"Nope." Jason shook his head. "Not going to happen."

"Pleeassseee."

"Okay, okay." With his free arm, Jason obliged and easily flexed his bicep, much to Kayden's excitement.

"One day will mine be as big as yours?"

He ruffled Kayden's hair. "Of course, because you'll be just like your Uncle Jason."

Hopefully not just like him, Jason thought ruefully. With any luck, Kayden would be happily married or at least find a nice girl to enjoy his life with. It was lonely to live the way he did. He ran a hand through his hair and forced the thought away. It was what he'd chosen. And he'd live with it. But just because that was his path, it didn't mean it was the kind of life he'd guide Kayden into.

Done with dwelling on his life choices, Jason swung Kayden around on his back, so he carried him monkey style. "Let's go have that soak now." He turned toward the hot tub, and his eyes locked with Lisa's. Had she been watching him? The sweet smile on her face told him she had.

Maybe he didn't have to live with his choices after all. Maybe there was time to make changes? The thought came out of nowhere and was so unexpected, Jason almost dropped his nephew. He didn't know whether it was the Lodge or the woman, but he hadn't felt so...so hopeful about anything in a long time. And he'd barely been there forty-eight hours, or had a conversation with her that didn't end with one of them frustrated.

Just imagine what could be if you let it, a little voice inside him said.

"Okay, buddy." Jason put Kayden down with a soft plop when they got to the hot tub. "Soak your feet, and then slowly slide into the water until your body is submerged."

"But not your head?"

"No." Jason laughed. "Not your head."

Kayden did as he was instructed, taking the whole process very seriously.

"Like that?" he asked as soon as his shoulders were under the water.

"Just like that." Jason smiled and closed his eyes before he slid in next to him.

"I saw you over there."

He'd expected the voice, or at least hoped for it when he'd set them down so close to her, but hearing it made him happier than he cared to admit because it meant she had noticed him. Slowly, as if it was no big deal, he opened his eyes and looked at her.

She was beautiful. Her long blond hair piled up on her head in a messy ponytail; her bikini top only enhanced the curves he'd noticed before through her uniform. She was definitely stunning. Especially without his cousin Conrad anywhere to be seen.

"Did you?" Jason replied with a slow smile.

The look she gave him in return was killer. Smoldering eyes bored into him, and he had to fight the instinct to reach for her and pull her close. Not only because it was a completely ridiculous urge to have considering they'd only just met, but because he was pretty sure he'd get slapped and his very young, very impressionable nephew sat very close by.

"I was talking to him." Lisa turned so her whole body was angled toward Kayden and very obviously, away from him. "You're a very good swimmer, Kayden."

"Thanks." Kayden sat straighter and pushed his shoulders back. "But not as good as my Uncle Jason. Do you know him?"

Her smile was sweet, and it was obvious she enjoyed children. She wasn't just one of those who pretended to like kids because that was their job; she actually did. "We've met."

She didn't even turn to him, which stung more than Jason cared to admit, but she was so charming and totally beautiful, that he brushed it off and watched as Lisa continued to engage Kayden in conversation, which he absolutely ate up.

"""Well, I think you're pretty good." She smiled and gestured with her head toward the other pool. The knowledge that she'd been watching them lit a fire deep inside him. Maybe this woman who pretended to be irritated by him actually liked him. Even a little bit. Or maybe it was his nephew she liked so much? Judging by the way she still ignored him and fawned over Kayden, that was more likely the case.

"Did you see my cannonball?" Kayden grinned proudly. "I'm going to be big and strong, like my uncle one day."

Lisa nodded, but still didn't look in Jason's direction.

"I'm going to have muscles like him one day." Kayden jumped up and pulled on Jason's arm. "Don't you think he's strong?"

She had no choice then but to look at him, and when she turned and met his eyes, he was positive he saw a flicker of something behind her gaze. Desire? Heat? Or maybe it was just irritation. It was hard to know.

But when Lisa's lips turned up in a smile and she said, "Oh I think he looks plenty strong," Jason had no doubt there was desire in her eyes or at the very least, a flicker of interest. And despite all the logic telling him he needed to walk away and leave her alone, he knew that wasn't going to happen.

Chapter Four

IT WAS Lisa's favorite part of the day. Only three kids were in the Cub Club so far, and while she knew there'd be more, she still had another hour before the chaos started. It was good chaos, and she loved every minute of it, but when the little room filled up with happy, excited kids, the noise level could rise exponentially. And for even the most dedicated worker, that could get exhausting.

She looked around the room. Two little girls and one little boy played with an animal set on the rug in the middle of the room. It was amazing how boys and girls could play together so well when they were little, and then as they got older, something shifted. Until they were her age, and she couldn't seem to be in the same room with a man and have a functional relationship with one. Not that she knew what a functional relationship even was, she mused.

She shook her head and focused on the tasks at hand. Which meant preparing for the hike they'd promised the kids. She scanned the table in front of her and the snack bags she'd had sent up from the kitchen. Morgan usually trusted her with most of the preparations for the outdoor activities, because even though she'd been at the Lodge for just over a year and dated the outdoors activities director, she still couldn't seem to fully embrace the outdoor lifestyle. Lisa laughed. And that was considered a functional relationship.

"What's so funny?" Morgan appeared by her side.

"Nothing. I was just thinking about how ironic it was that you're practically married to Bo, and you hate the outdoors."

Morgan picked up one of the snack packs and examined it. "I don't hate the outdoors."

"Okay, you distinctly dislike it."

Morgan laughed. "I'd like to think it's a little better than that. I've changed a lot in the last few months. I actually like hiking now. Just don't ask me to camp out," she added with a smile and they both laughed.

"I suppose everyone has their limits."

"That's exactly it. And my limits involve my own bed and indoor heat. Or at the very least, room service."

Lisa raised her eyebrows.

"And no, Bo bringing me coffee in a tin cup made over the fire doesn't count. Give me a hotel any day," Morgan added.

"Well, as long as it works for you guys," Lisa said. And it did work for them. They were one of the happiest couples she knew. Despite their differences, they made it work between them. Maybe it was because of their differences.

Lisa shook her head and concentrated on the task at hand. She had spent far too much time thinking about men and relationships in general for the last few days. It wasn't like her to give men more than a passing thought, and she'd promised Morgan. It was a promise she'd keep.

She looked over to where Morgan consulted a clipboard and checked things off a list.

"It looks like we're only waiting for four more kids today," she said. "It's a pretty small group. That's perfect because we won't need another adult. It's just the two of us."

"Sounds good to me."

They both looked over when the bell over the door rang.

A mother, with a timid little girl clinging to her leg, walked through the door. "I'll go get her checked in and settled." Morgan headed toward the door.

Lisa spent a few more minutes going over the checklist and made sure the first-aid kit was well stocked. When the bell over the door rang again, Lisa assumed Morgan was still there and would handle the check-in. She kept her head down and focused on what she was doing. The sooner they got organized, the sooner they could head out.

"Excuse me."

Lisa turned in the direction of the voice. A voice that made her pause and her stomach flip.

Jason.

Lisa glanced around quickly, and found Morgan sat with the little girl on the floor. She was obviously upset, and probably suffered from a bit of separation anxiety. Morgan looked up and gave Lisa a helpless look. Understanding, Lisa headed toward Jason and Kayden, who stood proudly next to him.

"Hi." She spoke to the little boy. "Welcome to the Cub Club. It's good to see you again."

"It's good to see you, too."

Lisa glanced up, annoyed, and saw a devilish grin on Jason's face. What was it with this guy?

"I was talking to him." She held out her hand. "Hi, Kayden. How are you doing this morning?"

"Fine, thank you." He nodded seriously; he'd obviously been taught very good manners. But then he turned and said, "Uncle Jason, she's pretty."

"Yes she is."

Lisa looked up and expected to see another grin on Jason's face. Instead, he had a straight face. Impossible to read. Lisa shook her head and focused again on Kayden.

"Are you ready for a hike this morning? It's going to be a beautiful day so we're going to head out on the trails and see if we can spot any animal tracks."

"Animals? Will there be bears?"

"There might be some, but don't worry, we won't see any. They don't like people, so they hide."

Jason rubbed the boy's head. "You're in good hands, buddy. And you're going to have way more fun than the adults. We're doing boring family talking and stuff." He straightened and handed Lisa some papers. "These are the permission forms from his mom."

"She didn't want to come?"

"I like to hang out with Kayden whenever I can," Jason said. "So I kind of take over. Is that okay?"

"It's fine," she said. "I don't usually meet uncles who are so involved is all."

"Well, you've never met me."

She had to give him credit; he was definitely coming on strong. And as much as she wanted to play along and flirt back, she didn't. She wouldn't. The last thing she needed in her life was a one-night stand. Especially with a guest who could cost her her job. Not even one she was as insanely and unexplainably attracted to as Jason. She took a deep breath and straightened her shoulders.

"Okay." She dragged out the word. "Well, I think the papers are all good. So you can sign him in here. And Kayden, you can go play until it's time to leave. There's lots of fun things to do. Do you like Lego?"

He nodded and Lisa pointed in the direction of the bin full of blocks.

Like most boys, he didn't need to be told twice. With only a backward glance toward his uncle, he took off, ready to play.

"So you can pick him up at three today," she said. "We'll feed him lunch since we're going on a hike."

"Sounds like a fun day."

Lisa focused on what she wrote on the clipboard, which was nothing of importance, but she needed something to focus on besides him. "It will be," she said without looking up.

"Do you do a lot of hikes?"

"Yes, we do." Lisa clipped her pen on the board and looked up sharply. "I really have a lot to do. Is there something else you need before you leave?"

His face changed. The smile faded a bit. "Look," he said. "I just wanted to—"

Before he had a chance to finish his thought, the door opened again with the last of the children they were waiting for. "I'm sorry. I have to take care of this." Without waiting for a response, Lisa turned her attention to the new arrivals, and out of the corner of her eye, saw Jason slip out the door. It wasn't until much later that she realized, with a twinge of regret, that she never did hear what he'd been about to say.

There was so much more he could have said. Should have said. But Lisa was so obviously uninterested in him. Hell, she was downright irritated by him.

Or was she?

He wasn't stupid; he'd been around enough to know when a woman was into him. And she was. Except she wasn't. And even if she was, what was the point? The last thing he needed in his life was another relationship—look at how the last one had turned out. Even if Nikki hadn't been in the car accident that day, he'd never have been able to ignore where she'd been coming back from that night. You just couldn't ignore that kind of thing. The fact of the matter was, with or without the accident, their relationship was over. The fact that she'd been killed on impact only complicated things. Especially his feelings. How did you grieve for someone who'd been deceiving you for months? She'd broken his heart, long before she'd died.

He made his way down the hall, and tried to process his thoughts. "Maybe Jen's right?" he muttered.

"Right about what?"

Dammit. He turned to see his twin sister grinning from ear to ear. "I'm always right. But what is it this time?"

He waited for her to catch up and they fell into perfect stride together as they made their way to the main lobby, where they were supposed to pick up an agenda with some of the day's activities.

"What do you think of me going to work for Porter Properties?" He totally changed tracks because as dangerous as it was to talk about the family business, it was less of a minefield than talking about relationships. Especially when both of them were completely dysfunctional.

Jen eyed him carefully. She was no fool, and she knew her brother better than anyone. There was no doubt that she wasn't going to fall for his lame distraction technique, but she didn't push it. "Why would you ask?" she said slowly. "You're not really considering it, are you? You know Dad would love it, but do not joke about it because the last thing I need to hear about is how you're teasing him with promises and then changing your mind. I really don't need that and if you even think about waving this in front of him and then running back up North, I will hunt you down and drag you back here." She narrowed her eyes at him and they both knew she'd follow through on her threat. Jennifer had been working in PR at Porter Properties since she'd graduated from college. She handled herself and the family dynamics beautifully, but she'd made it clear from the beginning that she didn't want anything to do with management. Of course that hadn't kept their father from trying to sway her, but everyone in the family knew it was Jason he really wanted to take over the business. And it was Jason who was the best suited for it.

If only he could be convinced of it.

And maybe he was. Time healed a lot of things, and maybe it was time to try something new.

"I was thinking of it." He watched his sister's face closely, but if she was surprised, she hid it well.

"Good." She continued walking, and Jason had no choice but to follow her.

"Good?"

"What did you expect me to say?" He knew she was playing with him, but still, he'd expected a little more enthusiasm out of her. Or at the very least, some sort of sharp comment about why it had taken him so long to smarten up.

"I guess I thought you'd tell me how smart I was and bow at my feet in gratitude or something like that."

He ducked swiftly but wasn't fast enough to miss Jen's hand as she spun around to smack him on the shoulder.

"What was that for?" He rubbed the spot, but couldn't hide his smile. It didn't matter how old he got; it was still good to know he could get under her skin. "I mean, I don't think it's asking too much for you to be in my debt for coming to save you."

She raised an eyebrow in his direction and rolled her eyes. "Actually, I don't think you should say anything yet."

Jason almost tripped over his feet. That was not the response he'd expected to his ribbing. "Wait. What?"

Jen stopped walking again and put a hand on her hip. "Look. I know you thought we'd all be jumping up and down at your announcement. Not that telling me is really an announcement. But..." She looked around quickly. "I just don't think it's a good idea to broadcast it yet. I mean, come on, Jason. Conrad will say something to make you mad, or push you too far, and you'll change your mind again. You're not ready."

He had to shake his head to be sure that he really heard what he thought he heard. Jen and the rest of the family had waited for years for him to be ready and now that he was, she told him he wasn't? He wasn't a little kid who was going to take his ball and go home if Conrad pissed him off. He was a grown man, for Christ's sake, making a career choice.

"I don't think you know what you're talking about."

She tilted her head and gave him a patronizing smile that she knew he hated. "Jason, you know I'd love to work with you and don't even get me started about how Dad's going to react. But do you really think you can work with Conrad? He's still the same jerk he was before, and you've never—"

"Don't, Jen." His sister was the only one besides himself and Conrad, of course, who knew the truth about Nikki. And no, maybe he hadn't forgiven Conrad yet. But he could get past it for the sake of the company. Couldn't he? "Don't use my past to determine my future. That's not fair."

For a minute, he thought she was going to push the issue, but she was smarter than that. Jason didn't often lose his temper, but he might if he was backed into a corner and Jen didn't deserve that.

"Well, why don't we go and test that theory?" Her face transformed into a devious smile and Jason instantly knew he wasn't going to like whatever it was that she suggested. She grabbed his hand and tugged him toward the lobby. "We have the whole day ahead of us, and that means there's a whole lot of family fun to be had. No time to waste."

Jason swallowed down a groan and trudged after her. After all, he really didn't have any room to argue. He'd swallow his irritation, put a smile on his face and prove to his sister that whatever happened in the past between him and his cousin was just that—in the past. Even if he wasn't so convinced.

With Morgan bringing up the rear, Lisa relished the opportunity to lead the children down the wooded path. She loved the outdoors, but even more, she enjoyed teaching children about the simple pleasures that being outside could bring. Kayden had become fast friends with Nate, a little boy about the same age. Together, they stuck close to Lisa, who entertained them with stories of the animals who lived in the forest.

"Tell us about the bears," Nate said.

Lisa purposely had avoided any mention of bears because Kayden seemed to be a little nervous about them earlier. She glanced in his direction. He didn't say anything but Lisa didn't miss the tension in his jaw as he listened carefully.

"There really aren't many bears here," she said. And then she darted forward on the trail and stood next to a tall yellow tree. "Do you know what type of tree this is?"

"It's a pine tree," Kayden said.

"Do bears eat them?" Nate peered around the tree, likely looking for something more interesting.

"It's not a pine tree," Lisa said. She focused on Kayden.

"But it looks like one."

"Yes, it does."

"Do bears climb them?"

"It's actually a really cool tree called a Larch. In the summer, it looks just like a pine tree, with needles and everything. But in the fall, it turns this beautiful bright yellow and loses its needles just like a leafy tree."

"That's cool." Kayden grinned. He looked at his friend. "Don't ya think?"

Nate shrugged. "Kinda. But I wanna hear about bears."

Lisa smiled and looked over at Kayden. Avoidance didn't seem to be working, so she decided on a new strategy: tell Nate just enough to keep him happy, but not enough to scare Kayden.

She glanced down the path where Morgan walked with the girls. She could hear the refrain of a song as it floated toward her. Morgan liked to sing with her hikers.

"Okay," she said. "But let's start walking again."

The boys fell into step beside her on the wide trail. "Well," she began. "There are bears in the forest. But don't worry. Because we don't see them very often. They don't really like people very much."

"They don't?" Kayden asked. His eyes were wide.

"No. They're actually quite shy, so we like to give them their space, too. Any guesses why?"

It was Nate who piped up. "So they don't eat us."

Kayden's eyes got even wider, if it was possible. "Don't worry." Lisa reached for his hand and gave it a squeeze. "Bears don't eat people."

"That's not true," Nate said. "I heard that a grizzly bear will—"

"They don't eat people," she said again. This time a little firmer. "But if they're scared or feel threatened, like any animal, they will attack. And that's why we give them space."

"Kind of like when my mom says she needs space," Kayden said.

Lisa laughed and swung his arms, enjoying their time together. He was a bright kid and even Nate with his questions and fascination with bears was a lot of fun. She couldn't have asked for better kids to hang out with.

"Hey," Lisa said. "We're almost at the lake. It's just a little bit farther and we can have lunch. Are you guys hungry?"

They both cheered and Lisa laughed again. Little boys were always hungry.

"Can we run?"

Lisa looked behind her to see where Morgan was. It looked

as if she was having a good time with the girls, who wandered their way up the path and looked at everything. Morgan waved Lisa on.

"Sure." Lisa let go of their hands so they could move faster. "Let's go on ahead and pick the lunch spot."

Nate and Kayden both cheered the way she knew they would, so she picked up the pace until they lightly jogged down the wooded trail.

It was only a few minutes before they broke through the trees and into a clearing where a beautiful glacier-fed lake dominated the landscape. She stopped an admired the view, the way she always did. It didn't matter how many times she saw Crown Lake—it always took her breath away. On the close end, where she stood with the boys, there was a dock that they used to launch the canoes, but the boats had been put away for the season already. Crown Lake was quiet at this time of year and the water was so perfectly still that the surrounding mountains almost had an exact mirror replica reflected in the water. She could have stared at the tranquil scene all day but she had little boys to watch, and sure enough, they'd already made a beeline to the water's edge.

"Be careful," she called. "The rocks are slippery and that water is cold."

That was an understatement. The water in a glacier-fed lake was just that: glacier cold. They'd been lucky to have such nice weather so far into the season, but Lisa knew it could snow any day and it wouldn't take much for Crown Lake to freeze over. It was one thing to look at the lake, but swimming was totally out of the question.

"Don't worry, we're just going to throw rocks." Kayden picked up a handful of stones and threw them one by one into the water and shattered the glassy calm of the surface. "I can throw farther than you can," he challenged Nate.

Soon both the boys were engrossed in a competition and

Lisa decided to set up the snacks she had in her backpack on a nearby picnic table. She pulled the granola bars out of the pack, and was just about to lay out the juice boxes when she realized the boys had become very quiet.

Quiet and little boys did not go together unless they were up to something. She whipped her head around as she chastised herself for turning her back in the first place. They'd given up on their competition and now balanced on the large boulders that bordered the water's edge and picked their way along.

"Be careful, you guys." Both boys froze and looked at her, legs poised midair. She left the snacks and started toward them. "Those rocks can be—"

A shriek split the air. Lisa burst forward, but there was no way she'd have been able to get to Kayden in time. He lost his balance and fell sideways into the water. It only took three steps to reach him, and in one fast move, Lisa gave Nate a shove back toward the shore and reached down to haul Kayden from the shallow water.

His eyes were wide with shock and he was soaked from head to toe.

"It's okay, buddy." She forced her voice to be calm. "I got you." She dragged him to the shore and immediately stripped his hoodie off. "Are you hurt anywhere?" She didn't think so; in fact, the fall wasn't high enough to do much damage, except for maybe a few bruises and of course, more dangerous, make him wet and cold.

Kayden shook his head.

"Good." Lisa offered him a smile she hoped was reassuring and called to Nate who stood, unmoving, and watched the scene unfold. "I need your hoodie, Nate."

"But I'll get cold." The boy wrapped his arms around himself.

"Not as cold as Kayden. I need your help, okay?"

Nate nodded, finally understanding, and shrugged out of his sweater. He handed it to Lisa, who tugged it quickly over Kayden's head.

"Are you okay?"

He nodded, but started crying softly. "I'm so cold, Lisa." Of course he was, and it was only going to get worse.

"I know, buddy." Lisa glanced around and searched for an option, but didn't find any. There was still no sign of Morgan and the rest of the kids. "Nate, I need you to go down the trail and find Morgan, okay? She won't be far and I need you to go tell her what happened."

It went against everything she'd ever been taught, to send a child on his own down the trail, but she didn't have any other choice. "Stay on the trail, Nate, and yell her name as loud as you can until you get to her, okay?"

He nodded and set off, set on his mission and ready to take it seriously. Lisa watched as he disappeared down the path. Morgan wasn't far, and she knew he'd be okay. Her first priority had to be Kayden and keeping him warm.

"Come on, Kayden. I need you to walk with me over here, okay?"

He nodded. Tears still streamed down his face and his chin chattered, clacking his teeth together.

Lisa moved him as quickly as she could to the shack where the lifejackets and supplies were kept for the canoes. She prayed it was unlocked, as there was no reason for anyone to break into the building so far up in the mountains.

With one arm wrapped around the shivering boy, she jiggled the handle and pushed against the door. To her relief, it opened with a crash and she shuffled him inside. Once out of the air, Lisa helped Kayden out of his soaked shoes and jeans and found an old towel to wrap around his waist. It probably wasn't the cleanest towel, but it was dry and that was far more important at the moment.

"I'm sorry, Lisa." The words came out in bursts as Kayden tried to control his shivering. He looked so sad and upset that Lisa's heart cracked a little.

"You're okay. I'm not mad at you." She rubbed his arms over the towel. "Accidents happen, right?"

He nodded and sniffed loudly. She kept talking to him, reassured him that everything was going to be okay. Pretty soon, Kayden calmed down enough to control his tears, although she would've been happier if he still wasn't shivering so violently.

There wasn't much more she could do, so Lisa wrapped her arms around him as tightly as possible and held him tight when Morgan burst into the hut.

"What's going on? What happened? Is everyone okay?"

"He's fine, Morgan. It was just a bit of an accident. He's just a little cold."

"Really cold," Kayden added.

"Really cold."

"We need to get him back," Morgan said. "Right away before it gets too cold."

"It's already too cold to go all the way back to the Lodge, Morgan. He'll never make it that far. Not without dry clothes."

"Okay, I'll stay with Kayden, and you can take the others back down the mountain to get help." Morgan took charge of the situation. "The others are just sitting outside having a snack. As soon as they're finished, you can go."

"There's only one problem with that plan."

Morgan turned and looked down at Lisa.

"As soon as the sun goes down, it's going to freeze in here," Lisa said. "And don't forget how early the sun goes down these days."

Morgan bit her lip and paced around the small room. "I don't know if we have another choice."

Lisa pulled herself away from Kayden and stood. She

gestured to the door and the two women slipped outside. The other children sat at the picnic table, a safe distance from the water, and peacefully ate their snack. "I have an idea," Lisa said when they were out of earshot. "Settler's Cabin isn't too far from here. Kayden's a good hiker, and we should be able to make it in about thirty minutes while the sun is still high enough not to be too cold. It's not ideal, but if he wears my sweater, it will be big enough to cover his legs. And once we get there, I can build a fire to dry out his clothes."

Morgan listened, and contemplated Lisa's idea. "I should be the one who takes him," she said after a moment. Lisa didn't say anything; she didn't have to. "But…you are better outdoors," Morgan added after a moment. "And Kayden really does seem to like you."

Lisa nodded.

"Okay," Morgan said after a moment. "It's the best plan we've got. And you're right; he'll never make it all the way down the mountain before freezing. Will you be able to get there fast enough?"

"I think so. We'll leave right away."

Not wanting to waste any more time, Lisa tugged her sweater over her head and shivered involuntarily at the sudden chill on her bare arms. They'd been lucky with the November weather. Very lucky. But there was no mistaking that winter was right around the corner. And she hadn't been exaggerating when she said they'd freeze if they didn't get to the cabin before dark. When the sun went down in the mountains, it got cold. Fast.

Chapter Five

THERE WERE a dozen different things Jason would have liked to be doing in the mountains, and playing games with the adult members of his extended family was not one of them. But he'd told his sister he'd be able to forgive Conrad, and he'd be dammed if he wasn't going to prove it. Even if the mere sight of him caused Jason's skin to crawl. Maybe he wouldn't be able to work with him. Maybe Jen was right and it was a bad idea.

Jason shook his head and grabbed a soft drink from the cooler before he headed back to the field, where an excessively competitive game of horseshoes was going on.

"Hurry up, Jason. It's your turn."

Jason lifted his hand in acknowledgement to his cousin, Chase, and made his way back to his teammate. At least he'd managed to secure himself a partner he wasn't likely to kill. Chase drove him crazy at times with the whole sense of entitlement thing he had going on, but he wasn't a bad guy and from what he could tell, he actually had a handle on his responsibilities at Porter Properties, and Jason could respect that. Even if his older brother was a total jackass.

He reached the pit and Chase handed him his horseshoes.

"Let's win this already. We only need one more point to shut these jokers down."

Jason took a quick glance toward his Aunt Betty, who raised her eyebrow at Chase's choice of words. "Done," he said with a wink in his favorite aunt's direction.

With a nod, Chase made his way back to his side of the pit. So far, Jason and Chase had managed to win three of their matches and were in contention to win the entire horseshoe tournament. Someone, likely his cousin Emily, had created a chart outlining all the games, the winners, and who would play who next. If Jason and Chase won this game against his Aunt Betty and her latest boyfriend, they'd be headed into the championship match against Conrad and Emily's husband Nolan. There was nothing Jason wanted more than to beat Conrad.

He lined up his shot and with a focused determination, he made his shot. The sound of metal connecting rang out as he made contact with the pin, but the shoe spun off the pin and landed in the sand with a thud.

"Dammit."

"Don't worry about it," Chase called from his end. "You got this."

Jason nodded and grabbed his soda while Aunt Betty lined herself up.

"You know, dear, if you just concentrated more you wouldn't have any trouble at all." Aunt Betty stopped mid-swing to impart her wisdom. For as long as he could remember, his aunt had been trying to "teach him a thing or two" about life. For the most part, it was entertaining and totally harmless, and at the moment when she was supposed to be concentrating on her own game, it had the added benefit of causing a distraction for her.

"Is that right, Aunt Betty?" Jason leaned against a nearby tree trunk and crossed his arms. "You know, I could really use a bit of help with my concentration. And you do it so well." If his aunt knew he was giving her a hard time, she didn't show it.

"Watch and learn, kiddo." Betty swung her arm back again to prepare for the shot. "It's all about focus. No matter what it is in life, if you have focus, you'll be fine." She released the horseshoe and they both watched while it flipped through the air, landing nowhere near the target pin.

Jason swallowed his laughter but couldn't keep the smile from appearing across his face. "Now that was impressive, Aunt Betty. I mean, you sure showed me how to concentrate," he teased her gently and she swatted him on the arm.

"Well, maybe it has something to do with aim, too."

"Maybe." Jason chuckled and lined up for his next shot. "But if it's all the same to you, I think I'll use my own strategy on this one."

She waved her hand at him and moved aside while he lined up for his shot. This time he didn't take long before he tossed the horseshoe, and he watched in satisfaction as it arced up and landed with a soft plop and a metal twang as it circled around the pin.

"Yes!"

Chase fist pumped the air and they each took a moment to celebrate their victory. The Porter family took their horseshoes very seriously, and a championship would definitely give them bragging rights.

"Nicely done, boys." Aunt Betty smiled and patted each of them on the back. "It's that throwing arm, Jason." She squeezed his bicep through his T-shirt. "If I had muscles as big as these ones, we'd be winning all the games, too."

"You did great, Aunt Betty." Jason put his arm around her and gave her a gentle squeeze. "But it's not the arm—it's the concentration, right?"

She smacked him playfully. "You're a feisty thing, Jason.

What you need is a good woman to keep you in line. When are you going to find a nice girl and bring her by for us to meet?"

Jason's thoughts immediately went to Lisa, which was beyond ridiculous considering she'd barely even spoken to him. But there was something about her, and he had a feeling she was definitely feisty enough to keep him in line. Maybe if he apologized for being a grade-A jerk when they'd first met, he could convince her to go for dinner with him? Maybe even a family dinner?

"Well, you never know, Aunt Betty. I might just bring someone around."

Why the hell had he said that?

"Oh really?" Jason spun around to see Conrad stood behind him. "And who would that be?"

Jason clenched his teeth and ignored the question. "I didn't realize eavesdropping was your thing now." Jason's hands automatically fisted and his entire body tensed. Conrad's presence had that effect on him.

"If you have a new lady friend," he emphasized the last words, "I think we'd all love to meet her." Conrad's voice slurred slightly and it took all Jason's control not to punch him. "After all, it has been awhile."

Jason lunged forward, but thankfully Aunt Betty stood between them, so Jason backed down. Just because Conrad deserved to be taken down a few notches didn't mean he was going to disrespect his favorite aunt to do it in front of her.

"Boys." She patted both of them on the chest. "This is a fun family event. Settle it over a game of horseshoes. It's a Porter tradition, after all."

"Sounds good to me." Conrad leered at him and took a swig of beer. By the look of him, it hadn't been his first drink.

Leave it to Conrad to get drunk at a family function. "We all know how this will play out."

Jason swallowed his rage and nodded curtly.

"We got this, Jason." Chase pounded him on his back and took him aside. "Don't let him get to you. Let's just win this."

Jason glanced behind him and saw Nolan walk up, ready to get the game going. Conrad crushed his now empty beer can and tossed it in the bushes. Anger flared through him. "Yeah, let's go win this."

As a matter of point, Jason returned to the side of the horseshoe pit he'd held earlier despite the fact that Conrad now shared that space. Maybe because of that fact. He wasn't going to back down from his jackass cousin; quite the contrary.

"Why don't you take the first throw?" Jason nodded in the direction of the pins.

"You think we need to go first? Because I don't need any kind of advantage, you know? I'll win this game with or—"

"Just throw," Chase yelled from the other end of the pit.

Jason tilted his head but didn't bother to hide his grin.

"Come on, Conrad," Nolan called. No doubt he was already sick of the cousin rivalry. He'd met Emily right before things had really turned bad between Jason and Conrad. Given that most people didn't know the truth about Nikki's deception, or Conrad's betrayal, most of the family couldn't understand the animosity between the two men. As kids they'd been so close; it was particularly hard for the older members of the family to see the rift that continued to grow. Most of the younger family members just got irritated, the way Nolan was now. "We don't have all day. Let's just win and move on."

For a moment, Conrad looked as if he was going to argue again, but finally he picked up his horseshoe and without much bothering to take his time to line up his shot, he tossed. Surprisingly, it landed with a thud fairly close to the pin. Closer than Jason would have liked.

Jason followed it up with an even better shot, which brought a grunt from his cousin.

Conrad took a bit longer to line up his next shot, but Jason's final throw was closer to the pin, and earned them the point.

With a curse, Conrad stomped off to the tree where he'd left his beer and cracked the top on another while he moved out of the way for Nolan and Chase to take their turn.

"Tell me about your girl," Conrad sneered as he came up beside him. Jason bristled, but chose to ignore him. He wanted Jason to lose his cool and blow up. He wouldn't give him the satisfaction. "I bet she's looking for a real man, too." Jason's hands formed fists at his sides. "It won't take much, either. It didn't take more than a touch and a promise of a night she wouldn't forget for Nikki."

That was it. Nikki was off-limits. No matter what kind of relationship Conrad may or may not have shared with her before she died, he had no right to so much as mention her name. Before he could stop himself, Jason swung around. His fist connected squarely with Conrad's jaw.

His cousin took two stumbling steps backward before he fell back into the dirt. His hand went to his jaw and he stared openmouthed at Jason, whose rage was only barely simmering. "Don't you ever mention her name again."

Conrad had the decency to look surprised, and maybe even a bit ashamed, but for Jason, it was too little too late. He swung again. This time Conrad blocked the punch. "JasonI don't know why I said—hey." Conrad dodged another swing. "Really, I'm—"

It didn't matter what Conrad had to say; Jason wasn't interested. He lunged forward and knocked his cousin off balance. They both toppled to the ground.

He didn't know how many hits he got in, and he barely noticed the sting of Conrad's own fist connecting with his face.

He was too consumed with the white anger that he'd somehow managed to put a lid on for the last four years.

The fight didn't last long enough as far as Jason was concerned before Nolan's arms pulled him off and shoved him backward. "What the hell is wrong with you? Em would kill you if she saw you. Never mind Jen—"

"Let me go!" Jason twisted out of Nolan's grip and wiped his lip. His cousin's husband was right. Jason had no business getting in a family fight. Even if Conrad had deserved it.

Without looking back, he turned and prepared to walk away.

"Hey."

There was something in Conrad's voice that stopped him momentarily, but he didn't turn around, and when Conrad yelled, "I loved her, too," Jason gritted his teeth, clenched his fists, felt the sting in his knuckles, and stormed off.

Fortunately for both of them, Kayden was very brave and considered their departure from the rest of the group as an adventure. Lisa used it to her advantage and turned their short hike into a fun adventure. Despite his great attitude, he was young and cold, and the hike took him a lot longer then she'd hoped. With any luck, Morgan had made better time than she had and was already down the mountain with the others.

The cabin was always locked, although Lisa wasn't sure why. Fortunately, she knew the key was hung on a nail on the side of the window frame. She quickly unlocked the door and ushered Kayden inside.

"What do you think?"

"Cool. Does anyone ever stay here?"

Lisa walked through the room and opened the shutters to let what remained of the sunlight to shine into the small space.

Consisting of one main living room that had a small kitchenette along the back wall, the cabin wasn't much, but it was perfect for the overnight excursions that some of the guests of the Lodge liked to participate in. Two small bedrooms were equipped with bunk beds, so the cabin could sleep up to eight people, ten if you put them on the couches. Regardless, it would be more than enough for Lisa and Kayden to stay warm until help came.

"Well, we're here," she said. She pulled two big blankets off one of the overstuffed couches that surrounded the fireplace, and handed them to Kayden. "Here, wrap yourself up and stay as warm as you can. I'll dry your clothes."

Kayden did as he was told. "But we don't get to stay, right?"

Lisa glanced outside at the quickly dimming light. "You know what? I think we might get to extend our adventure a little bit longer, after all. It's getting dark, so it's probably safer to stay here. And, more fun, right?"

"Yeah." Wrapped up in a blanket, he wandered around the room. "It's cool here. Like camp. But better."

"It is pretty awesome here," Lisa agreed with a smile. "I like to come whenever I get a chance. Hey, have you ever made a fire before?"

Kayden shook his head.

"Well, how about you help me, and I can teach you some things? Does that sound okay?"

He nodded eagerly and joined her close to the fire.

"Okay," Lisa said. "But you have to stay back. No closer than this." She threw a pillow on the floor. "But I need you to help me with the kindling. To make a good fire, we need kindling. Do you know what that is?"

Kayden nodded and then shook his head. "Not really."

Lisa laughed at his eagerness to please. He was such a sweet boy. "Kindling is the little bits of wood, dry grass, and other things we can burn that will start the fire fast. If you look at the bottom of the wood bucket here, I bet you can scrape up enough to help me start a good fire. I'm going to look for a little paper that can help us light it."

Lisa left Kayden happily digging through the bucket and making piles of straw, wood shavings, and twigs. She puttered around the kitchen and located cans of soup and an unopened package of crackers. It was the makings of a good dinner, because it was looking more and more like they'd be spending the night. There was no way Lisa could take him down the mountain at night, especially with his clothes still damp. That, and he was just a little boy. He was likely to be exhausted with all the hiking they'd done, not to mention the excitement of falling in the lake.

It would be best to get him fed and warm so they could both fall asleep and get an early start in the morning.

"How are you doing over there?" She rejoined him and put the paper in a pile next to his kindling.

"I think I have enough." Kayden waved his hand over his collection. "Do I?"

Lisa smiled and ruffled his hair. "It looks good. I think we should be okay." She moved over to the firebox and pulled out some of the smaller sticks. "Okay, we have your awesome kindling, and some paper and of course the sticks. We should be able to get started."

Kayden looked on with hero worship in his eyes as Lisa deftly made a teepee style fire stack, and explained what she was doing the entire time. She even let him reach in and lay on one of the sticks before she had him retreat to the safety of the pillow. Once he was settled, Lisa pulled out the long stick matches, lit one and put it to the paper in the center of the teepee, where it caught immediately.

"Awesome."

Lisa looked over at Kayden, who had a huge smile on his

face, and laughed. It was easy to forget the magic of fire when you were an adult. Looking at it through the eyes of a child made her remember how great it could be. Yet another reason she loved hanging out with children.

"So now all we need to do is add some larger pieces of wood, and then the fire will really catch hold and we can just enjoy it." Lisa looked into the woodpile again, but it was a little low on the bigger logs. She'd have to go outside to the woodpile. "Hey, buddy. I'm going to get you to sit up here on the couch for me while I go outside, okay?"

Kayden immediately did what he was told. She smiled. He was such a good kid. She worked with a lot of children, some better than others, but Kayden was definitely one of the sweetest and smartest. Not to mention one of the best behaved.

"I promise, I'll only be a few minutes and I'll be right outside, okay? But I really need you to stay up here away from the fire, okay? I know it's cool but it can be really dangerous if you're not careful."

He nodded and looked serious enough that Lisa believed he'd be fine.

The second she stepped outside, she took a big breath and filled her lungs with air. It was beautiful up at Settler's Cabin, and she hadn't been lying when she said it was one of her favorite places to be. Soon, the snow would fall and she wouldn't have nearly as many chances to get up there. So despite the less than perfect situation that had brought her there, she might as well enjoy it while she could.

The woodpile was around the back of the cabin, so she took the basket from the front porch and made her way down the steps. Maybe in the morning she'd be able to take Kayden down to the falls before they headed back to the Lodge. She dismissed the thought the moment it popped into her head.

She knew she'd have to take him back the moment the sun came up. His family would be worried about him, as she was sure she would be, too, if the roles were reversed.

Not that he wasn't safe. They were perfectly safe up there. But that wouldn't be enough to alleviate a mother's fears.

Lisa knelt down and gathered wood, and filled her basket. A snap and a rustle from the front of the cabin caught her attention, but she didn't move. She may have played off the threat of bears when she talked to the children, but it was a very real threat up so high in the mountains, especially as the animals prepared for hibernation. Slowly, Lisa picked up the biggest stick she could and turned around, ready to go defend herself and Kayden from whatever animal had wandered near.

In one move, she leapt to her feet and snuck to the side of the cabin, ready to scare the animal. She turned the corner and brandished the stick over her head. She let out a scream that would have been enough to scare all the birds from the trees.

She lunged forward and almost smacked into a large man. She lowered the log, but didn't drop it.

"What the–"

"Whoa—"

"What are you doing here? You scared the life out of me."

Jason stood in front of her, his hands outstretched to fend off imminent attack and a grin on his face. "I came to rescue you," he said.

Lisa lowered the stick and put her other hand on her hip. "I do not need rescuing." She glared at him. "But you might." She swung the piece of wood again before she dropped it into her basket. "Seriously, how did you get up here so fast?"

She gathered up her basket and walked toward him, a wary expression on her face. "Morgan couldn't have been back for long. And it takes awhile to hike up here. You must have been flying."

"Something like that." Jason gestured to a mountain bike in the yard. "I was out for a ride and I ran into Morgan halfway up the trail. I didn't see any point in wasting any more time, so I thought I'd come straight up."

From the look of his sweat-ringed T-shirt, he'd worked hard to get there so quickly. Lisa tried not to notice his hard chest, and the way the cotton clung to it. She cleared her throat and looked away.

"Besides, I thought you might need—"

"To be rescued?" She spun around again and raised her eyebrow at him. "Because I'm perfectly fine. You know, I do know what I'm doing."

"I'm sure you do. I wasn't trying to imply you weren't, but Morgan made it seem like it was an emergency situation. Is Kayden okay?"

"He's fine. He slipped in the lake and got wet. We couldn't have made it all the way back down without him freezing to death. Besides, it's kind of an adventure for him." She stopped in front of Jason and looked him in the eyes, trying to ignore the spark she felt when she did so. "He's pretty excited about it."

"I bet he is."

He held her gaze for a moment and looked as if he was going to say something else, but when he didn't, Lisa moved to push past him. "Well, we should get in there then. I told him I wouldn't be gone long."

Lisa had to slip sideways to move past Jason, who didn't get out of the way to let her by. When her still bare arm touched him, shivers went through her, and she didn't think it was because of the rapidly cooling air. "Wow," she said. "It's starting to get cool out here."

Jason smiled, but didn't say anything.

When she opened the door to the cabin, she looked first to the fire and then to the couch, where Kayden was still curled up. He looked as if he was almost asleep, but his head popped up when he heard her.

"You're back." His voice was so eager, Lisa's heart melted a little.

"I told you I was just going outside. And look who I found out there." She stepped aside to reveal Jason, who was still in the doorway.

"Uncle Jason." Kayden leapt off the couch and ran to his uncle, who picked him up and wrapped him in his arms.

"Hey, buddy. I heard you were a bit clumsy today."

Kayden nodded. "I slipped. But it's okay because we got to come up to this super cool cabin and we couldn't have come if I didn't."

Jason put him down and tried to look stern. "Maybe," he said. "But your mom is going to go crazy with worry. We should call them."

"Oh," Lisa said. "I don't have a radio."

Jason pulled one from his pocket. "I do. They gave me one when I insisted on going out on the bike alone. They wanted to send me with the outdoor guy—"

"Bo."

"Yeah. Bo. But I kind of insisted I wanted to be alone." He shrugged casually, but by the look of him, and the cut over his eyebrow that looked like it would leave a bruise, Lisa was pretty sure there was a reason he wanted to be alone. "So I guess it all worked out," Jason finished.

Kayden cheered and Lisa tried to ignore the way her stomach flipped. "Probably a good idea." She reached out for the radio. "I'll go in the other room and check in. I suppose you'll be staying then?"

"Staying?"

Jason left Kayden on the couch and moved to the back of the small space where Lisa stood.

"We'll have to stay the night." Lisa felt suddenly claustrophobic by his large presence in the cabin. "I found a bit of food for dinner and we'll—"

"We can't stay."

Lisa swallowed her disappointment that he wanted to go. "Well, we can't leave." She put her hands on her hips and stood up straight. "It's going to be dark soon and Kayden's clothes aren't dry. We're staying."

"His mother will flip out." Jason shook his head. "I love the mountains, and I'm always up for an adventure." Had he just raised his eyebrow at her? Lisa tried to keep her face neutral. "But Jennifer thinks the mountains are full of danger. She'll lose it if Kayden stays up here."

"There's no other choice." Lisa tried to take a step back, needing distance between them. "I'll try to explain it to her."

"I don't—"

"Can we stay, Uncle Jason?"

They both swung around to the voice.

"It's fun here. And Mom won't mind. Not if you're here."

Jason turned and looked at Lisa again. Knowing she'd won, she tried not to smile.

She failed.

Chapter Six

JASON WASN'T DISAPPOINTED at the idea of staying the night in the cabin. Far from it. He loved the mountains. In fact, there was a time when he would have said that they were second only to the company of a beautiful woman. That time was long ago, but being up at Settler's Cabin with Lisa felt right. Even if she did challenge everything he said. The truth was, it had been a long time since he'd enjoyed spending time with a woman and the little he knew about Lisa, he liked. A lot. He was determined to spend more time with her and being stranded at a remote mountain cabin couldn't be more of a perfect opportunity.

She'd gone into the back room to radio down to the main Lodge, and Jason used the opportunity to clean up his face a little bit at the sink. After he left the horseshoe pit, he'd needed to be alone and work out some frustration. The best way to do that was by working up a sweat and he'd more or less bullied the poor girl who rented the bikes out to let him go out without a guide. The fact that he likely looked as if he'd taken a beating probably had a little something to do with that.

The fact that Conrad had to be in worse shape brightened

him considerably as he dabbed at his sore lip. There was running water in the sink that looked to be piped in from the nearby creek. It was primitive, but it worked and soon he'd washed up and hoped that he looked to be in better shape than when he'd arrived.

Interesting that Lisa hadn't commented on his face. Either she didn't care, or she was trying not to attract attention to it. Jason chose to believe the latter. Because if she didn't care that would mean that whatever attraction he could feel growing between them was completely one-sided. And that wasn't an option.

The strength of that thought surprised him. Was it even possible that Jason liked this girl? Like, really liked her?

He shook the thought clear and went to check on Kayden. He stared into the fire and was almost asleep on the couch, so Jason didn't disturb him.

"Jason."

When he turned and saw Lisa in the doorway, the radio in one hand, his breath caught momentarily in his throat. The light from the room glowed behind her, highlighted her blond hair and cast her face into an elegant shadow. He moved toward her, certain she was going to tell him a secret or something.

"Yes?"

"Your sister is waiting to talk to you." She thrust the radio at him. "Just push the button in and speak."

He took the radio clumsily. "I know how to work a radio."

She smiled and gave him a wink that caused a tug low in his groin. "Good. I'll go start dinner." She slid past him, and it took all of Jason's self-control not to wrap his arm around her waist and pull her close. He could hardly believe the thoughts that flew through his brain when it came to this woman. It was so unlike him that even he had a hard time understanding it. He watched her as she walked to the small kitchen and opened cupboards. With a shake of his head, he turned and retreated to the bedroom.

"Jen. Come in. This is Jason."

His sister's voice came across the radio. "Jason. You're both okay?"

A smirk crossed his face and he pressed the button. "Copy that. Kayden's fine. Sleeping right now."

"Oh thank God." He could hear the relief in his sister's voice, and his heart swelled a little. He couldn't imagine what it was like to have a little piece of your heart walking around outside of your body the way Jen had Kayden. "They said Lisa was great and—"

He pressed the button early and cut her off. "She is great."

There was silence on the other end and Jason wondered whether she'd heard him at all. Finally, he said, "We're fine. We'll be home tomorrow."

"Good." Silence again, but he could still hear her breathing. "And Jason?"

Something in her voice told him exactly what she was going to say next. "Yeah."

"What was that with Conrad? You can't do that."

"Do what?" He knew damn well what she was talking about, but the last thing he wanted to do was get into it with Jennifer when Lisa waited for him in the next room. Waited for him. That was a thought. But Jason wasn't stupid enough to think Lisa actually waited for him. She was there for Kayden. The fact that Jason happened to crash their overnight adventure was a minor detail that nobody had planned for. Not that he didn't intend to make the best of it. Because damned if that woman didn't make him feel something again.

"I know," Jason finally managed to respond to Jennifer. "I'm sorry. I hope it wasn't too big of a deal after I left." Truthfully, he didn't care whether the beating he gave Conrad caused any trouble or not. And he wasn't really sorry. And both of them knew it, which was evident by the long sigh Jennifer let out.

"There was drama," she said. "You had to know there would be."

He nodded a moment before he depressed the button to speak again. "Sorry."

"But you must have gotten some good shots in." He didn't miss the note of pleasure in Jen's voice. "He was a mess."

Jason smiled and pressed the button again. "He deserved it."

"That's what Chase said."

That came as a surprise. Chase usually stuck with his brother. It wasn't very common for Chase to say anything against Conrad. Especially where Jason was concerned. "Is that right?"

There was a moment of silence before Jennifer's voice came across again. "That's what he said. But I don't want to know what happened or what Conrad said, because I'm pretty sure I have a good idea."

"You do."

He could hear Jennifer's sigh as if they were in the same room. He knew she was tired of the constant feud, but he couldn't seem to let it go.

"You need to stop, Jason. It's not worth it anymore. The past is just that. In the past. It's time to start living again." There was a pause and Jason couldn't think of anything to say to fill it. "Just take care of Kayden, okay?"

"You know I will."

"I do."

"We'll be back in the morning. Don't worry."

"I will. But it helps that you're with him. Goodnight, Jason."

He signed off and took a minute before he joined Lisa and Kayden in the other room. He knew his sister was right. She always was. He needed to let it go. Whatever happened with Conrad and Nikki was a long time ago. Even if she hadn't been killed in the accident, their relationship was over and they'd both known it. He wasn't without fault, but blaming Conrad for everything that had gone down wasn't the answer.

The sound of dishes came from the other room and Jason smiled. It was time to think of the future, and that's just what he intended to do.

She would have loved to hear what Jason had to say to his sister on the radio, but Lisa wasn't about to eavesdrop. Besides, he was probably busy trying to reassure her that Kayden was okay and they'd be perfectly safe at the cabin. The conversation between them likely didn't have anything to do with her at all. But there was a little part of her—okay, a growing part of her—that couldn't help but hope he talked about her. There was something about Jason that she couldn't get out of her head. It was the way he looked at her, as if she was the most beautiful woman he'd seen, the way he cocked his head when she spoke as if whatever she said was fascinating. It had been a long time since she'd felt like that with a man. Or really, felt like that at all.

When she'd spoken to Morgan on the radio, she had half expected her friend and boss to tell her that she was sending up a crew to take them home. Lisa had done her best to reassure her that everyone was okay and Kayden was safe and dry, and really, the best thing for everyone was that they stay where they were for the night. More than being at the cabin and enjoying the solitude she felt there, Lisa couldn't help but want the time alone with Jason. She'd been pleased, if not a little surprised, when Morgan agreed with her about staying.

Kayden was thrilled, and excited about the adventure, the

way Lisa knew he would be. And even though Lisa was pleased to have Jason with her, she still wasn't totally sure about him. He'd been so hot and cold with her since they'd met. Maybe she was wrong about the underlying feeling she got from him. And even though she tried to relax and be herself, when Jason showed up the dynamic had changed a little bit. Suddenly, she wasn't as sure about being herself. She was instantly on edge and afraid she'd do or say the wrong thing.

She couldn't figure him out. At times he pulled back, and closed up with her and yet, he'd still flirted with her, and more disturbing was the way she responded when he did.

She tried not to think about it, and told herself she would be herself without question, no matter what. If Jason didn't like her, that was his problem and if he did—well, she'd figure that out later. It's not like anything would come of it anyway. Lisa stirred the stew again. Instead of cooking over the fire the way Kayden wanted, she'd opted to use the little camp stove they kept in the cabin, with the assurance that they could roast the marshmallows she'd discovered in the cupboards over the fire.

The back door opened and Jason appeared. He gave her a slight wave and her stomach flipped a little, like a school girl. She forced herself to ignore it. "How did it go?"

Jason glanced over to where Kayden poked at the fire with a stick Lisa had given him. He was being good and stayed a safe distance away from the flames, so Lisa let him be. For a moment, she thought Jason might tell him to stop playing with the fire, but to her surprise and secret delight, he smiled and watched for a minute before he changed course and moved across the room to stand next to her. "It went well." He leaned up against the counter, and put his arms behind him. Lisa tried not to notice the way his arms bulged and his hard chest strained against his T-shirt. "Jen's not happy about it, but she knows Kayden is safe and more than that, he's excited to be here. Even if he does look ready to fall asleep."

"I'm not sleepy." Kayden put the stick down and looked at both of them, a look of pure determination on his face. "This is great. I'm not sleeping. Ever."

Lisa laughed. "I believe you, buddy. But why don't you lie down on the couch for a few minutes until dinner is ready. I promise I won't let you sleep."

He looked as if he was going to argue with her, but after a moment, he nodded and did as she suggested. The poor kid must be exhausted, but he didn't want to miss a second of the night. She smiled to herself and chuckled a little.

"What's so funny?"

The smile melted from her face and her shoulders straightened. "Nothing."

She didn't look at him, but she heard him push off the counter and cross the small distance so he stood close to her. Very close. She could feel the heat from his body, and smell his earthy scent. "Seriously." His voice was softer. "What's funny?"

She turned to look at him. His proximity took her off guard. He didn't seem to be making fun of her, or trying to rile her up. In fact, there didn't seem to be anything antagonistic about the question at all. So she answered him. "I was just thinking about how sweet it was that Kayden is obviously asleep on his feet, but he—"

"Doesn't want to miss anything?" Jason smiled as he finished her thought. "I was thinking the same thing. He's pretty pumped."

She nodded and turned back to the stew.

"That's all thanks to you. You're great with him," Jason said. "He can't stop talking about you. I was trying to get him to play cards with me earlier and all he can talk about is, 'Lisa this…Lisa that.'"

She blushed and shook her head. "That's not true at all.

The only thing that little boy can talk about is his awesome Uncle Jason."

"Well, you're in good company, then."

Lisa automatically shrugged away from him and his flirtation. She'd never pretended to understand men, but with all his mixed signals, Jason was one man she really couldn't understand. And there was no point trying. Even if she did feel a strong pull to him.

"Dinner's ready." She ducked around him. "Kayden, are you hungry?"

The little boy lifted his head from the couch, where he looked to be almost asleep. "Yup."

"Come and—"

"Let's eat—"

Jason looked to her and gestured for her to continue.

She frowned. "Come and wash your hands before you eat."

"Good point," Jason whispered in her ear. "I didn't think of that."

"Well, it is my job." She had to twist to the side to slide past him in the small kitchen, but suddenly the room seemed even smaller and she needed her space.

Lisa handed Kayden a steaming bowl before she joined him on the couch again. She left Jason to get his own. She was saved from making small talk with him because Kayden dominated the conversation by reliving his day, including a play-by-play of his slip into the water.

When he finished eating, and talking, Lisa couldn't decide who was more exhausted. Just listening to him had worn her out. "Alright, kiddo," she said. "I think you should get tucked in so we can get an early start in the morning."

"Aw, can't we stay?"

"Sorry. I'm sure your mom will be missing you and it wouldn't be fair to the other kids if you got to have all the fun, right?"

Kayden nodded in agreement, but he didn't look convinced.

"Hey, buddy," Jason chimed in. "You've already had a pretty awesome extra adventure, don't you think?"

"Yeah, but…"

"Maybe," Lisa glanced over at Jason to gauge his reaction, "we'll have time in the morning for me to show you the really cool waterfalls that are out here. Maybe."

Jason smiled and gave her a slight nod. She returned his grin.

"Really?"

"But first, you sleep," Jason said.

"And you have to promise not to fall in."

Kayden opened his mouth to protest, but Lisa ushered him into the back bunk room. "I'll get him settled," she said behind her.

Jason didn't protest, which was good because even though he was Kayden's uncle, she still felt responsible for him, and the last thing they needed was a power struggle. Especially considering she was having a hard enough time getting a read on Jason and whether he liked her, or whether he just couldn't wait to get out of the cabin and away from her. Maybe it was the whole new approach she was taking with men that muddled everything up? That was probably the entire reason she was having such a hard time navigating the situation. But she was serious about her new resolve. If Jason, or any man for that matter, was going to be interested in her, he was going to be interested in the real Lisa, not some attention-seeking flirt. And if all he wanted was a fling, she was the wrong woman. Her stomach flipped at the thought that he might want more. She pushed the feelings aside, and filed them under totally ridiculous ideas.

She tucked Kayden in and hadn't even left the room before she heard the telltale sound of deep breathing that told her he'd already succumbed to sleep. After she checked to make sure the window was locked tight, she had no other reason to procrastinate, and she went back to the main room.

"Hey."

"Hey yourself," she said.

Jason sat on the floor in front of the fire, which blazed brighter now. "Is he asleep?" She nodded and Jason chuckled. "Well, that didn't take much, did it?"

She leaned up against the wall, not sure where she should sit. Without Kayden, the atmosphere between them had become significantly more awkward. "He was pretty tired."

"You can sit down, you know? I'm not going to bite."

Lisa shook her head at her own ridiculousness. He was just a guy and no matter what their feelings were, they were both stuck at the cabin at least until morning, so she might as well try to make the best of it.

"That's a no?"

"No," she said. "I mean, yes. I wasn't shaking my head at you. It's me." She crossed the room, and slipped down to the floor next to him. She picked up a pillow and leaned against the couch. "I was just thinking of something. Sorry."

He smiled and looked back to the fire. The silence grew between them, but it wasn't weird this time. They both looked into the flames, and Lisa let her thoughts drift off. She loved Settler's Cabin and the Lodge, but the unsettled feeling she'd experienced for the last few months returned. Even the mesmerizing flames licking against the logs didn't soothe her. Unwittingly, she sighed.

"You okay?"

She pulled her knees up to her chin, dropped her head

down on them, and peered at him from the side. "I was just thinking."

"About how nice it is up here?"

"Yes. And no." She stopped herself from telling him more. She had no business opening up to this man who was, for all intents and purposes, a total stranger. "Don't worry about it."

"Are you sure? I'm a good listener."

"Yeah, right."

"Hey." He sat back on his hands and stretched his broad and incredibly muscular chest out. "I am," he said. "And I know I haven't really given you much of a reason to think so, but I promise I'm not always a jerk."

"Just to women you don't know who work in childcare?"

"Fair point. I was an ass when we first met, with the whole…"

"Proposition thing?"

Jason groaned and smacked his hand in what she had to admit was a very cute and disarming gesture. "Yes, I was a total ass."

Lisa nodded in agreement.

"You don't have to agree with me."

"Hey, I don't argue with the truth." She ducked her head so he couldn't see the smile on her face.

"Seriously," Jason said. Something in his voice made Lisa sit up and pay attention. "I'm sorry for how I treated you. It wasn't fair. The truth was, I don't know why I said that to you. You kinda threw me off guard."

Were her ears deceiving her? Did he really just apologize? She tilted her head and examined him for signs that he was fooling with her. When she couldn't see anything but sincerity on his face, she swallowed hard. "I threw you off guard?" The idea was crazy. And how could she tell him that a few months ago, his comments wouldn't have been out of line and she didn't have the best reputation at the Lodge for her behavior with men? She couldn't. She took a deep breath.

"You did." He ran his hand through his hair and tipped his head back slightly, as if trying to figure out what to say. "The thing is, I don't really have relationships, and—"

"Well, I've decided only to do relationships." The words popped out of her mouth before she could think them through. "I deserve better than one-night stands." It was as if saying the words out loud helped affirm them in her head.

For a moment, she wasn't sure he was going to say anything. He didn't take his eyes off her, and they seemed to bore into her and see through the veneer she'd put on.

"You do," he said quietly a moment later. "You deserve much better than that."

His words caused a shiver to race up her spine.

"And you didn't deserve the way I treated you," Jason said. "Especially since from the moment I met you, I wanted to know more about you."

Lisa blinked and digested his words. "But then…why?" She shook her head. "I don't understand men. I thought I did, but…"

"Maybe it's simple men you understand." His words teased, and she saw the laughter in his eyes. "And I am not a simple man."

"No." She laughed to hide the increasing nervousness. "That's the truth."

Jason slid closer to her, and instantly her entire body was alerted to his proximity. Their bodies were only inches from touching, and Lisa couldn't help but wish he'd move just the tiniest bit closer.

"And besides the fact that I'm not a simple man, I'm actually a very perceptive man."

"Is that right?"

"It is. For example, I noticed the way that most of the time you try not to flirt with me, but fail miserably." She opened her mouth to protest, but he continued. "And the rest of the time, you treat me like even if I was the last man on earth, you wouldn't give me the time of the day. Yet, I can't help but notice the way you're looking at me now."

Reflexively, Lisa ducked her head, but after a second she lifted it again and met his intense gaze with her own. "You noticed that, did you?"

He nodded.

"I, too, am also very perceptive," Lisa said. She enjoyed their little game more than she cared to admit. "And I've noticed a few things of my own."

"Well, by all means, share."

She smiled and bit her bottom lip. "For one thing, I've noticed that from the moment I stopped giving you any attention at all, you've been flirting with me."

He nodded.

"And," she continued. "Despite the fact that you appear to be fairly intelligent, you don't seem to get the hint that I'm not interested."

She swallowed hard, unsure whether she should have added that last fact, because as the seconds ticked by, she meant it less and less.

"Okay." He shocked her by rocking backward and jumping up to his feet. Instantly, Lisa cursed herself and wished she could take back her words. "I'll explain that," he said. "But first, let's see if there's anything to drink in this place."

She watched while he moved across the room and rummaged through the cupboards.

"There might actually be a bottle of wine," she said. "Sometimes the guests like to have wine with dinner. It's the end of the season though, so—"

"Got it." Triumphant, Jason produced a bottle of wine.

While he wrestled with the cork and searched for glasses,

Lisa turned her attention to the fire and lost herself in the dance of the flames. She was more confused than ever. Nothing about their conversation made sense. Did he like her or not? More importantly, did she like him? Everything she'd thought was true wasn't.

He handed her a tumbler full of red wine, saving her from her thoughts. "Okay," she said before she lost her nerve. "What's going on? I don't like playing games, Jason. When I like a guy, I tell him. I don't know what's going on here, and I don't like it one bit, so—"

Her protests were cut off by his warm lips on hers. He gently reached around her, took the glass from her hand and with his free hand, pulled her closer to him. His lips gave her the answer she needed. Lisa was the first to break the kiss and pulled slightly out of his reach.

"That doesn't clear anything up," she said. Although judging by the way her body sang from his touch, she wouldn't protest if he did it again. Not at all.

He grinned and sat back. "Fair enough."

She waited while he picked up his glass and took a sip of wine. When he stuck his tongue out to lick a stray drop from his lip, Lisa almost caved in and kissed him again, uncaring about the why or what of the situation. But she held firm and crossed her arms around herself to keep from giving in to temptation.

"The first time I saw you, I thought you were stunning." Lisa felt the blush start at the roots of her hair and flood her face. "But then you opened your mouth." She sat upright, the blush replaced by an indignant glare. He laughed and she only glared harder. "Just listen." He held up his hands in defense.

"You're not funny."

"Anyway." He watched her closely. "As I was saying. When you opened your mouth and I heard how feisty you were, and saw the way you were with kids, well...suddenly you became the most beautiful woman I'd ever met."

Lisa melted a little at his words, and thought maybe if he didn't lean over and kiss her again soon, she might burst into flames. But then, Jason continued talking. "But I wasn't lying when I said I wasn't really looking for anything right now because that's my standard answer. But the truth is..." He paused and Lisa knew there was more. Much more that he didn't say. "The truth is, I've been burned. Badly."

Jason hadn't intended to tell her anything about his past. But sitting with her in front of the fire, being close to her, it felt right. And he actually wanted to talk about Nikki and her deception because it was time. It was long past time.

He took another sip of wine and turned to her. "I was engaged to be married before."

Lisa didn't even try to hide her surprise, which he appreciated. But she didn't say anything and let him finish what he needed to say, which he appreciated more.

"I thought she was the love of my life but in retrospect we were too young. There were a lot of things wrong with the relationship." He looked into the fire. "A lot."

"So you ended it?"

Jason shook his head. "She died."

Lisa sucked in a gasp and held her hand to her mouth. Instantly, he felt bad and the last thing he wanted was her pity. Especially considering he no longer mourned her loss.

"I'm so sorry, Jason." Her hand clasped around his arm. Her touch was warm and comforting and he covered her hand with his own, reluctant to have her pull away. "That's terrible to lose your wife so—"

"It was." He nodded. "But that wasn't the worst part."

Jason braced himself for what he was about to tell her. In the years since Nikki died, he hadn't actually spoken about her betrayal with many people. Jen knew, and of course Conrad. But other than that, no one knew the truth. "She'd been cheating on me." He said the words in a rush, and the instant they were out, he felt the pressure that had built for years release. It felt good, more than good, to let it go. "The night she died, she was coming home from her lover's house. It was late; there was an accident and—"

"I'm so sorry, Jason." Her hand moved from his arm, and cupped his cheek. "That shouldn't have happened to you. No one should have to experience that kind of pain."

He knew just by looking at her that she wasn't talking about her death, but her affair, and in that moment, he thought he fell for her a little bit harder. This woman got it. She understood instantly what had taken him years to understand.

"I can't even imagine what that was like. To grieve for someone who'd hurt you so badly. No wonder you're—"

"What?" He took her hand from his face and held it in his own much larger one while his eyes locked on hers. "No wonder I'm what?"

"Hurting," she said without hesitating. "I knew from the moment I met you that there was something else going on. Now I know."

She did indeed. And she wasn't running. She didn't look at him like a man who needed pity, or should be tiptoed around. Not at all. In fact, when Jason looked into her eyes, there was no trace of any of that in them. Instead, she looked at him with desire and respect. He traced her jawline with one finger and pulled her closer with his spare hand.

"I was," he said after a moment. "For years I was angry and I'd sworn off women altogether. I moved up North and I basically put my life on hold."

"What changed?"

You, he thought, but didn't say out loud. It was ridiculous that after knowing her for only a few days he should feel so totally reformed and deep down, he knew it wasn't Lisa single-handedly who had affected the change. But regardless, she'd played a role. If only for opening his eyes to see what he was missing and what he could have if he just allowed himself the opportunity to be open.

"It was time," he said simply. "It was just time to let it go and move on."

Her smile was sweet and Jason wanted to kiss her again. He needed to feel that sweetness on his lips again. He reached for her and tried to pull her in close, but she held back.

She shook her head slightly by way of explanation. "I need to be clear," she said after a moment. "I'm not okay with one-night stands, or quick affairs and I know that's all you do, so…whatever this is…well, just know that."

Jason swallowed hard. "When I first met you, I was drawn to you and like we've already discussed, I acted like a jerk more as a defense than anything else. It was safer that way." She nodded, understanding completely. But she looked down and wouldn't meet his gaze, so he tipped her chin up so she looked at him again. He needed her to understand it all. "But there was something about you. Every time I saw you, I knew there was something special about you, and I wanted…no, I needed to know more. And then when I saw the real you, I—"

"The real me?"

"Well, yeah." A smile split his face thinking about it. "When I saw you with Kayden and the other kids. I was just so blown away that everything I thought about you, women, and relationships went out the window, and I can't even begin to explain it. I can't help it."

"You can't help what?" She asked the question, but she was pretty sure she knew the answer.

He put his hands on her knees and closed what was left of the gap between them. "I can't help thinking that I want to get to know you better."

This time when he leaned forward and his lips met hers, he was ready for the way his body responded to her. He pulled her in closer and let his mouth express what he couldn't with simple words.

Chapter Seven

WHATEVER HAD HAPPENED between them had definitely caused a shift and it wasn't just the kisses. But as Lisa pulled away from Jason's embrace, needing a bit of air so she could compose herself momentarily, the urge to lean right back in for another kiss was strong. More than strong. She'd never felt a pull toward a man the way she felt toward Jason. And it wasn't just physical. There was something about the way he sat and listened to her, and especially, the way he opened up to her. She could tell he'd never talked to another woman about his past before. And that made her feel special. Very special.

Lisa wasn't in a hurry for the evening to end and so instead of giving in to their growing exhaustion, they talked through the night. Going to sleep would break the spell of the evening and it was only when Lisa saw the sky outside start to lighten that she insisted they close their eyes for a bit. Even if it was only for a few hours. The connection they had shared and whatever it was that was happening between them was strong, Lisa was sure of it. She'd never felt such a way about a man. And despite the possibility of breaking the spell, she had to take the risk and get a little rest.

Despite being wound up and having just had the best evening she'd had in years with a man she'd just met and kisses to end all kisses, Lisa fell into a deep sleep almost the moment she laid her head on the pillow and closed her eyes. Unfortunately, there wasn't much time for sleeping before Kayden ran through the cabin in an effort to wake them both.

"Come on, Lisa," he said when she gave in and opened her eyes. "You said we could go to the falls in the morning. And it's morning."

"I said we could go if we had time," she mumbled, and rubbed at her eyes.

There was no point trying to go back to sleep. Lisa knew enough about small children that once they had their minds made up about something, there would be no rest for anyone who didn't go along with their plans.

"Come on, buddy." Jason walked into the room. His eyes landed on Lisa, still lying in her bunk. "We should probably let Lisa get organized. Don't worry; there'll be lots of time to go to the falls."

"Really?" Kayden jumped up and took off before his uncle could change his mind.

"Really?" Lisa asked. She raised her eyebrows in question, but gave him a little grin.

"That is, if you think we have enough time," he added, not taking his eyes off her. "Because I'm not in a hurry to get back."

"You're not?"

Jason shook his head slowly. "Not at all."

She looked into his eyes and in that instant, she knew that everything they'd shared together the night before was still there. The reality of the morning hadn't changed anything.

After a quick breakfast of some cereal bars that Lisa found in the cupboard and some instant coffee for the adults, they did a quick cleanup of the cabin and were on their way. The falls were only a short walk and with an energetic and fully rested little boy to lead the way, it didn't take long for them to reach their destination.

"Now, Kayden." Lisa crouched down in front of the boy. "I know you're excited, but do not go anywhere near the water. If you slip in again, we'll be back at the cabin." Lisa paused at the thought of having to spend another night with Jason, away from everything and everyone. She glanced up and met his gaze; by the look on his face, he obviously had the same idea. She turned back to Kayden. "And we can't do that. Your mother would flip out."

Kayden nodded solemnly. "I'll be careful."

"Okay." Lisa stood and ruffled his hair. "If you go over to that side there," she pointed to a big rock, "you can sit on the edge and feel the spray. You might even see a rainbow in the water."

"Really?"

She nodded. "But be careful."

"I will," Kayden promised as he ran off.

She shook her head, but couldn't help smiling. He was a great kid and it was nice to see children so enthusiastic about the outdoors. Besides that, it was perfectly safe where she'd sent him. He'd be fine.

Lisa was so busy watching Kayden that she hadn't noticed Jason slide behind her until his arms were wrapped around her waist. She let out a little gasp of surprise as he pulled her into his chest.

"I didn't mean to scare you." He dropped his mouth to her neck, and gave her a little kiss while he squeezed her tight. "I've been wanting to do that since I saw you looking so cute, all rumpled up this morning."

She twisted in his arms so their faces were only inches apart. "Did you?"

"You know I did." He leaned in to kiss her and despite the

shivers of anticipation that raced through her, Lisa deftly dodged him.

"We can't."

His face fell and she couldn't help it; Lisa's heart jumped at the thought that he was disappointed in more than missing out on a kiss. "Not because I don't want to," she said quickly. "But not with Kayden around. It's too confusing for kids and especially if we don't even know what this...and I'm working," she finished lamely.

Jason opened his mouth to say something, but he closed it again and nodded solemnly. "Okay."

When he unlaced his fingers from around her waist and stepped back, Lisa immediately wanted his arms around her again. Instead, she settled for sliding her hand into his and gave it a quick squeeze. He smiled at her and winked at her to let her know that he totally understood.

Lisa's stomach flipped the way it always seemed to when he looked at her that way. It was unbelievable to her that in all her adult years she'd never felt such a way around a man before, but after only a few days of getting to know Jason, she felt like she'd known him forever.

"Uncle Jason! You've got to see this."

Lisa smiled and gestured to Kayden, who sat the way he was supposed to on top of the rock on the far side of the falls. "You better go see." She smiled and gestured toward the boy.

"You should come, too."

"I've seen it before."

Jason's smile melted her and caused a pooling of liquid heat deep in her belly. "Not with me you haven't." Her hand still in his, he tugged on it gently until she walked with him. There was no way she could argue with that logic, nor did she have any desire to do so.

The hike down the mountain back to the Lodge went quickly. Too quickly, as far as Jason was concerned. He could have spent all day in the mountains with Lisa and Kayden. She was great with him, singing songs, and pointing out wildlife, different late season wildflowers, and all kinds of things that Jason never would have noticed. As he watched her, he couldn't help but be impressed with the way she interacted with Kayden. She'd be an amazing mother one day. The thought popped into his head and surprised him. Where had that come from? He'd never before thought of children, at least not beyond Kayden. And he'd certainly never thought of children with another woman.

Jason shook his head and forced himself to slow down. Kissing Lisa may have felt good. Really good, but a kiss was a far cry from children, especially with a woman he'd just met.

As soon as they cleared the tree line and walked into the open field behind the lodge, Kayden broke into a run. Suddenly the little boy who'd been so excited to go on an overnight adventure was more than ready to get home to his mother. Of course, his mother would have been feeling the same. Just as he'd expected, Jen waited for Kayden. Lisa stopped walking and Jason came up to stand next to her. Both of them watched the mother and son reunion.

"Wow," Lisa whispered. "That's really…"

"Special?" Jason finished for her. "Their bond is special. It always has been."

"I suppose all bonds between mothers and their children are special, but…"

He turned to look at her as she drifted off. He couldn't be sure, but it looked like a wistfulness filled her eyes. "Did you want—"

"Jason!"

He jerked away from Lisa toward Jennifer, who held Kayden's hand and waved in his direction. He took one last look at Lisa, determined to finish the conversation later, and with a jerk of his head, said, "We should go."

Jen met them halfway across the field; Kayden bounced next to her. "Thank you." Jen reached for Lisa's hand. "You must be Lisa. I wish I would have had a chance to meet you earlier, but after only a few seconds with Kayden, I feel like I've known you forever. He can't stop talking about you."

"Lisa's awesome."

"She certainly is," Jason agreed. Jen gave him a sidelong glance, and he knew he was going to have to explain something later, but suddenly Jason didn't care.

"She knows everything," Kayden said. "She told me about plants and animals and did you know that bears are more afraid of us then we are of them? Did you know that?"

"I'm not sure that I did, Kayden." Jen smiled at Lisa, who blushed and shrugged.

"It's easy to teach so much when I have such a great student." She ruffled his hair. "You were great out there, Kayden. A real natural in the outdoors. It was a lot of fun spending the night at Settler's Cabin with you." She glanced in Jason's direction and he had to fight to keep from pulling her toward him and tasting her lips again. "But maybe next time you should try to stay out of the lake, okay?"

"Okay. Thanks, Lisa."

"No. Thank you." She smiled and glanced around. Her gaze landed on some movement by the lodge. "I should get going. I see my supervisor, and I need to fill her in. I'll see you later, okay, buddy?"

"Okay."

"It was nice to meet you, Lisa." Jen clasped the other woman's hand and pulled her into a quick hug. "I don't know how to thank you."

"It was my pleasure." Lisa looked embarrassed, but it was so cute on her, Jason was pretty sure he'd like to see her blush some more. "Honestly. There's no need to thank me. But I really should go."

Before Jason could stop her or make up an excuse to keep her there with them, she headed off across the field, with not much more than a wave in his direction. It wasn't a problem. He'd find her later. And maybe he would have a date to invite to a family dinner, or even the Porter Party. When he'd spouted off to his Aunt Betty about it, he'd just been shooting his mouth off, but all at once the idea of bringing a date to the dreaded family function looked a little more like a reality. A reality he'd be happy to participate in.

"What's going on there?"

Jason spun around and stared at his twin. "What are you talking about?"

Jen's face told him without a doubt that she didn't buy his playing dumb act. She knew him too well for that.

"She seems nice."

"I told you, she's awesome."

They both laughed. "She does seem awesome." Jen smiled at Kayden, who was ready to list off all of Lisa's positive traits again. "Why don't we go inside and get you cleaned up? We have more family fun later."

Jason's groan earned him a smack on the arm. "And we'll be talking later," Jen said to him. "Because I think there's a whole lot you need to tell me about."

He watched as his sister and nephew made their way across the field, hand in hand, and into the lodge. They walked right past Lisa, who still talked to her supervisor. They'd been joined by others, though. And from a distance, Jason couldn't be sure who they were, but as he walked closer, his blood ran cold.

Just like the other day in the pool, Conrad sat close to Lisa. Far too close. His hand inched closer to hers; his body leaned in to her personal space. His space.

A growl ripped through Jason's body, and his fists clenched

at his side. Lisa wasn't Nikki, he told himself. And he had no claim on her. He had no right to be angry if Conrad flirted with her. He forced himself to relax; the muscles in his body slowly released their tension. But as soon as he'd talked himself down, a familiar sound split the air.

Lisa laughed. The sound hit him deep in the gut, especially when he saw the way she flipped her hair back over her shoulder. He could only imagine the smile she gave him. The smile that should have been reserved for him. That only a few hours ago *had* been reserved for him.

By instinct, Jason stalked toward them and closed the distance between them with only a few strides. It didn't matter that he didn't hold a claim over her, and that he had no idea what it was that was going on between them. None of that mattered, because at that exact moment, all Jason could think of was history repeating itself, and he'd be dammed if he was going to sit back and watch that happen.

"Hey cousin."

Jason's fist ached to punch the sleazy smile right off Conrad's face.

"I was just telling Lisa here about the traditional Porter Party."

"Were you now?" He kept his gaze locked on Conrad, afraid to see what might be on Lisa's face. "I don't think she'd be interested in a stupid family reunion party."

"I don't know about that," Conrad said. "I suggested that maybe she come."

Jason worked double time to keep his face neutral. "I don't think that's a good idea. It's a family thing." He didn't know why that had come out of his mouth. Only a few minutes ago, he'd been thinking of what it would be like to walk into the party with her on his arm.

"I already asked her." Conrad's smug voice broke through his thoughts. "And she said yes."

Jason's head whipped around to stare at Lisa.

"Well…I didn't say…I said it sounded like fun. I didn't—"

"I hope you enjoy yourself then." Jason spat out the words like a spoiled little boy; he spun on his heel and left them both behind him. If she wanted to go to the party with his cousin, then who was he to stand in the way? He'd sworn that he wouldn't let history repeat itself, and even if it meant leaving an aching hole in his gut, he wouldn't put himself through that type of pain. He couldn't do that again.

Chapter Eight

ANYTHING WOULD HAVE BEEN a letdown after the adventure Lisa had with Jason and Kayden, and maybe that's what Morgan must have thought when she gave Lisa an unexpected day off for the following day. Instead of enjoying the time away from work, however, Lisa woke up at dawn and after trying desperately to occupy herself in her apartment with some of the chores she'd put off, she found herself outside, walking toward the main Lodge.

She knew she shouldn't go into work. She wasn't really needed anyway. According to Morgan, they had a pretty small group coming in and after all the excitement on their hike, Morgan was definitely not in a hurry to take the kids outside. She probably had a full day of crafts and inside games planned and Lisa knew if she popped in, she'd get sucked into the games and she'd never be able to go check out the main building. Which, if she was honest with herself, was the whole purpose of her walk.

She wanted to see Jason. No, she needed to see him. After their night in the cabin, talking and getting to know each other, she couldn't seem to stop thinking about him. Sure, the kisses they'd shared hadn't hurt either. In all her years, and all the kisses she'd had, none of them came close to what she'd experienced with Jason. That type of chemistry couldn't be faked.

But something was off, too. After they'd returned and Lisa had debriefed Morgan on everything, she'd wanted to talk to Jason again, but he'd seemed angry with her and distant. Cold even. She'd replayed the scene over and over in her head, and for the life of her, Lisa couldn't seem to figure out what could have happened to change Jason's impression so quickly. He'd made it very clear that she wasn't welcome at their traditional family party, not that she was really going to go. Not from Conrad's request. She had no interest in him. In fact, he kind of creeped her out a little. But if Jason himself asked...well, that would be different. But he most definitely hadn't. If anything, he'd made it very clear that he didn't want her there. Which meant that something must have happened between the time she left him and the time she walked across the field. Maybe it had been something his sister had said?

The thought stopped her in her tracks. A bird chirped somewhere in the trees next to her, but she barely noticed, focused as she was on that thought. When she'd gone to talk to Morgan, she'd left Jason and Kayden with Jason's sister. She'd seemed friendly enough to her, but what if she'd noticed the closeness between Lisa and her brother and hadn't liked it? What if she'd said something to change the way Jason felt about her? It was likely since she'd been spending time at the Lodge that Jen had overheard something about Lisa's past reputation. And if she'd told Jason that...well, Lisa didn't want to consider that as a possibility. But there was really no other. Everything had been going so well between them until then, even though Lisa had tried to tell herself Jason was probably just tired and had a lot on his mind.

But Lisa started to walk again, this time slower, as she made her way to the Lodge. She couldn't shake the feeling that it had been something Jen said to him that had changed things. And if it was about her reputation, there might not be anything she could do to change his mind. But that didn't mean she wouldn't try.

The main hall of the Lodge bustled with people coming and going, headed to activities and some even relaxed in the chairs by the fireplace with a small fire in it, probably mostly for ambience than anything else. Usually November was a slow season for Castle Mountain Lodge, but the new customer service director, Ryan Morrison, had made a few changes when he came in and by the look of things, they'd all been positive ones.

Ryan stood at the front desk, so Lisa made a point to go say hi. He'd replaced Carmen Kincaid, who'd been the longtime customer service manager at the Lodge. Carmen had been loved by everyone and was seriously missed ever since she'd decided to move to the new Springs resort her boyfriend Dylan Harrison had started a few hours away. Because of the big shoes he had to fill, Ryan was still trying to carve out his place among the Lodge staff.

"Hey," Lisa said as she walked up. "Working on some new and exciting plans, I assume?"

Ryan put down his pen and smiled. His face lit up and the dimple in his left cheek was more pronounced. Lisa knew a lot of the single women were interested in him, and she probably would have been, too, if she hadn't have sworn off men. But that was before Jason. She was so busy daydreaming about Jason, and the way his eyes crinkled in the corners when he smiled, that she missed what Ryan said.

"I'm sorry, what did you say?"

Ryan laughed. "I was just telling you about the idea I had for a masquerade ball for Valentine's Day. But if it doesn't hold your attention, maybe it's not a good idea." He blushed a little, but his eyes challenged her.

"No." Lisa waved her hands. "I'm sure it's a great idea. I'm just a little preoccupied is all. I have a few things on my mind."

"Yeah, I heard about what happened up at Settler's Cabin yesterday." He leaned up against the counter and Lisa didn't miss the fact that he was definitely flirting with her. She took a step back and crossed her arms over her chest, hopefully giving him the subtle signals that she wasn't interested. "That was some quick thinking up there with that kid. Good job. Morgan said you were absolutely fantastic."

"I don't know about fantastic." She smiled as she thought about Kayden. "I just did what anyone would have done. And it's not like it was a life-or-death situation."

"It could have been."

She shrugged. "Probably not. Besides, Kayden's a great kid and he made it a lot of fun to spend the night up there." And his uncle too, she thought but didn't say.

"His uncle joined you, too, didn't he?" Ryan asked as if he read her mind. "I was thinking of presenting them with a special family stay at the Lodge because of what happened. Maybe even at their big party that they have tomorrow night. What do you think? You could present it."

Lisa could feel her face heat up. Of course she wanted to go to the party, but not as an employee. She wanted to go with Jason. As his date. "I don't know…they don't really seem like—"

"Isn't that him there?"

Lisa spun around to see Jason as he walked into the reception area from one of the back doors that opened out onto the courtyard. He looked so casual and at ease in his faded jeans and buttoned-up plaid shirt. He looked like he fit perfectly in the mountain life. And hers.

She felt Ryan come up behind her and put his hand on her

shoulder. "It's usually good customer appreciation to do things like that. You don't think they'd like it?"

Right then, Jason looked up and his eyes locked with hers. Reflexively, she smiled. Just seeing him did that to her; she was like a little girl with a crush. But Jason didn't smile; in fact, his face turned down into a scowl and he quickly turned around, ready to walk back out the door.

Lisa's stomach fell. Whatever it was that was going on, she hadn't imagined it. He definitely wasn't the same man she'd left the night before. But she'd be dammed if she would sit by and let the strongest connection she'd ever felt with a man slip away without a fight.

"You know what, Ryan?" She slipped away from his touch. "I think I should go talk to him and get a feel for the situation. I'll let you know if I think they'd be open to it."

Before Ryan could say anything else, Lisa moved away from him and toward Jason, who had already left out the door. She broke into a slow jog. She wasn't going to let him get away so easily.

Jason exhaled hard and forced his breathing to slow down. It had taken all night to convince himself that Lisa wasn't interested in Conrad, and that his cousin's flirting had no effect on her. But maybe it wasn't his cousin he needed to be concerned with. Maybe it was Lisa. He knew it wasn't fair of him, but when he walked into the Lodge and saw that man with her—the laugh on her face, the smile in her eyes—he couldn't help it. His fists had reflexively clenched, itched to strike out. It was best if he just left. And quickly.

His entire body had yearned to go to her, pull her into his chest and claim her mouth with his own. But his mind, and the memory of being hurt before, stopped him. He hated it. But seeing her with Conrad and having her accept his invitation to the Porter Party was more than he could handle. The fact that she could do that to him after the time they'd shared together, it was too much.

No. He wouldn't do it again. Even if it meant walking away from the best thing he'd found since…well, ever.

"Jason!"

Lisa's voice rang out, and he stopped, frozen in mid-step.

"Jason." She was ever so slightly out of breath, and he could feel the small puffs of air on the back of his neck when she came up behind him. But still he couldn't make himself turn around. He knew he was being childish, but he couldn't seem to stop himself. Her arm clamped down on his and she turned him. "Jason."

Finally, he looked at her. She was hurt. He could see it in her eyes. *Well, good.* The feeling rose up in him before he could tamp it down again. He didn't mean it—he didn't want her to be hurt or upset—but dammit, he couldn't help it.

"What's going on?"

The flare in her eyes made her even more attractive, but still he held firm. Determined to guard his heart.

"I don't know what you're talking about?"

Her face fell and she dropped her arm. "Why are you being like this? I don't understand. I thought we—"

"Maybe you thought wrong." He regretted the words the instant they were out of his mouth. Whatever it was she thought about them, it wasn't wrong. He knew that much for a fact but he couldn't seem to stop himself. "Or maybe I was wrong."

Lisa took a step back as if she'd been struck. Jason caught himself seconds before he reached out for her. It hurt, and it sucked, but he needed to do it.

She opened her mouth but closed it again before she spoke. Finally, she spun on her heel and ran off. Instead of heading for the main lodge, she ran down the path that would take her toward the playground and small pond he'd found earlier in the courtyard. Every fiber in his body wanted to chase after her, pull her in his arms and kiss her until the hurt look he'd seen on her face, the one he'd caused, was gone for good. He never wanted her to be sad, or hurt, especially if it was because of him.

"Dammit." Jason kicked a rock.

"What?"

Jason spun around. "How do you do that?" Jen stood behind him, having come from where, he wasn't sure. He did a quick scan for Kayden, who was nowhere to be seen. "Where's Kayden?"

"I didn't do anything." Jen put her hand on her hip. "And Kayden is with Emily, which you should be thankful for because he does not need to hear his uncle using that language."

Jason shook his head but wouldn't meet his sister's eyes.

"What's going on, brother?"

"Nothing."

"That nothing wouldn't have anything to do with Lisa I just saw running away from here, would it?"

"It has nothing to do with you, Jen," Jason growled, and kicked another rock. "Stay out of it."

She laughed and Jason spun to stare at her. "Oh, I think it's plenty of my business when my twin brother finally falls for someone again and then for some stupid reason decides to sabotage what could be a very good thing just because he's scared."

Anger flared up inside him. And something else: realization. "I'm not scared."

"Then what is it?"

He couldn't answer that question. He looked down again, unwilling to look in his sister's eyes, and lie to her. Because he was scared. Scared of getting hurt again and for some reason that fear became crippling. He knew he was being a jerk with Lisa. He knew that even if she was talking to Conrad, and even if she was smiling while doing so, she wasn't Nikki. She wasn't going to hurt him like Nikki had. His brain knew that. He just had to convince his heart of it.

Jen put her hand on his arm, and he looked at her. "She's not Nikki." Jen spoke the words softly, as if not to scare him. "You have to open yourself up again, Jason. It's okay."

With nothing else to say, Jason pulled away from his sister and walked away. He needed to clear his head, and the best way he knew how to do that was with a walk in the woods.

Lisa ran around the corner of the building, desperate to put some space between her and Jason and his totally unexplainable behavior. She'd always known men were difficult, but for just a moment, she'd thought she'd actually found one who was different. She'd let herself believe that maybe there was a chance for her to have a real relationship with a man who saw her as more than just a dumb blond. And the second she'd opened herself up to the idea…

No. She wasn't going to dwell on it. She couldn't.

As she approached the pond in the center court of the resort, Lisa slowed down and wiped her hands over her face. A woman sat on the edge of the pond, absentmindedly rolling a stroller back and forth next to her.

Andi.

She'd forgotten that Morgan said Andi and Colin would be

coming to visit to introduce everyone to their new baby. Lisa had never been as close to Andi as Morgan or some of the others, but still she liked the kind, sweet woman quite a bit. Andi and her best friend, Eva, had become a fixture at Castle Mountain Lodge with their event planning company, Party Hearty. They frequently planned large events and parties and even when she was pregnant, Andi could often be found organizing weddings and large parties. Maybe Party Hearty was doing the Porter Party? She had no business thinking of Jason's big family reunion party. She would definitely not be there, not even to present an award or a gift, or whatever it was that Ryan wanted to give them.

Regardless, her curiosity won out. Besides, she did want to meet the baby. "Andi?" She interrupted the woman's peace and quiet before she could stop herself. Andi turned around and her face split into a smile. "Sorry to bother you."

"Not at all." Andi didn't get up, but she held her arms out for a hug, so Lisa bent and wrapped her arms around her. "It's nice to see you. Do you have a minute to chat?"

"Of course." Lisa had nothing but time now that her plans of talking to Jason had gone up in smoke. She slid down on the rock next to Andi and dangled her feet over the water. "It's really good to see you again. How have you been since…"

"You mean since my life totally changed in every possible way?" Andi laughed, but Lisa could see the exhaustion in her eyes. "Don't get me wrong, I love being a mom, but wow. I don't think you're ever prepared for how everything gets tossed upside down."

Lisa smiled. She didn't have any idea. She'd never actually given much thought to marriage or children. Not really. "Can I see…" She trailed off, as she realized she didn't even know whether Andi had a baby boy or a baby girl. She'd been so wrapped up in her own life that she hadn't paid any attention.

Andi didn't seem to hold it against her. "It's a girl." She

pulled the cover down off the stroller, and Lisa sat up enough to peek inside. "Her name is Lily."

Lisa was mesmerized by the cherubic sleeping face. Her delicate eyelashes fluttered in her sleep; her perfect little Cupid's bow lips seemed almost squished under her chubby cheeks. "She's perfect," Lisa breathed. She could have stared at the baby all day, totally entranced as she was with the precious bundle in front of her. "I…just…wow."

Andi laughed and Lisa reluctantly tore her gaze away from the sleeping child to look at her friend again. "Sure, she's perfect now. Wait until she wakes up and wants to eat. That is a girl who knows exactly what she wants, when she wants it. Colin says she's just like her mother."

Lisa couldn't help but chuckle at that. The two of them had a perfect relationship. At least everyone else thought so. Colin and Andi had a reputation of being the poster couple for Castle Mountain Lodge. A true romantic love story. Not wanting to wake the baby, she sat down next to Andi again.

"It seems like you have everything, Andi. Really." Lisa could hear the wistful note of longing in her voice as she spoke. She never would have guessed that she'd be wanting the happily ever after that Andi and Colin had. But something had shifted, and suddenly it was something she wanted more than anything else. "You're pretty lucky," she added.

"I am," Andi agreed, and Lisa appreciated the fact that she didn't sugarcoat it, or try to downplay things for her benefit. "But what about you, Lisa? How are things with you?"

"They're great." It was Lisa's pat answer, but it sounded dull on her lips. Things weren't great, but she didn't think Andi would see through her lie. "I love it at the Lodge. And working with the kids? It's great."

"Great." Andi repeated her word and it sounded just as disingenuous coming out of her mouth, but she didn't push it.

They sat in silence for a moment before finally Lisa asked, "Did you ever think you'd find love the way you did, Andi?"

The other woman turned to her. A smile tugged at her lips. "Not for a moment. But that's the thing about love, Lisa. You don't have to be looking for it. It finds you. And sometimes, like with Colin and me, it happens in the most unlikely way. You just have to be open to it."

Lisa thought about that for a moment. "Open to it," she repeated.

"Honestly, that's the key right there. Just look at all the couples who've come out of Castle Mountain Lodge. Colin and me, Eva and Jeff, Morgan and Bo, Carmen and Dylan..."

"Megan and Gage," Lisa finished for her, thinking of the movie star she'd tried to force herself on. She hadn't been able to make love happen for her then, but she knew now it hadn't been her time.

"I didn't know them," Andi said. "But yes, them too. All of those couples had one thing in common."

"Besides the Lodge?"

Andi's smile was genuine. "Yes, besides the Lodge. They were all open to the opportunity. None of us ever expected to leave Castle Mountain in love, but when the situation came up—"

"You were open. It sounds so cliché."

Andi nodded and laughed. "It's cliché for a reason."

"But how did you know Colin was the one?" The conversation was resonating, but there were still so many questions Lisa had. So much that still had to be explained. "How did you know he was the one worth being open for?"

Even as Lisa asked the question, she knew what Andi's answer would be. She knew the answer because it was the same answer she had for herself when she thought of Jason. And when Andi smiled and opened her mouth, she only reaffirmed Lisa's thoughts.

"You just know."

The two women sat and chatted for a while longer before Lily stirred. Andi stood and rocked the stroller back and forth, and settled her for a moment.

"This will only last for a few minutes," she said. "When she gets hungry, that's all she can think of."

"No problem. I should get going anyway." Lisa pulled herself up and brushed off the bottom of her shorts. "But it was good to see you, Andi. Thanks for the talk."

Andi pulled her in for a quick hug and squeezed. "Anytime. And remember, whatever or whomever it is you're questioning, cliché or not, stay open."

Shocked that she'd seen right through her, Lisa yanked backward and saw the sparkle in her friend's eye. She knew. Lisa nodded. "I will."

"And hey." Andi started to roll the stroller away, but before she went too far, she turned back. "Ryan said you were going to present an award or something at the Porter Party tomorrow? Party Hearty is doing the event. I thought I might turn it into a bit of a business trip while I was here."

She'd been right. A party at the Lodge that size, any size really, was a Party Hearty event. "Ryan was wrong…I'm not… I can't—"

The baby's cry split the air. "Well, that's my cue." Andi laughed, but Lisa could see the harried look in her eyes. "I'll see you later, Lisa."

After Andi left, Lisa actually felt a little better. She sat for a few minutes longer and dangled her feet over the edge of the pool before she finally decided to get up and go back to her apartment. Maybe she could change and go for a small hike?

She wasn't going to waste her day off thinking about Jason and things she couldn't change.

She was halfway down the path when a voice calling her name stopped her. She turned with a smile on her face as Kayden ran toward her. She opened her arms just in time to catch the little boy, who crashed into her.

"Hey, kiddo." She ruffled his hair. "How are you doing today?" His mother, Jen, joined them, a grin on her face as well. She looked so much like Jason it was impossible to look at her without thinking of the way he rejected her.

"Good," Kayden answered her. "Can we go on another hike?"

"No." The women answered in unison before they laughed.

"I think we're going to keep you close to home base from now on," Jen said. "Hey, do you mind heading inside to the lobby and finding Auntie Emily again? I wanted to talk to Lisa for a minute."

Kayden looked between them and gave Lisa another quick hug before nodding. "Alright. I'll see you later, okay, Lisa?"

"Absolutely."

The women watched as Kayden bounced off in the direction of the main lobby. "I keep thinking I don't want to let him out of my sight, but I know he'll be okay going inside."

Lisa nodded, sympathizing with her. "It must be hard after what happened. But I promise you, he was safe the entire time. Even when he fell in the water, he was—"

"Oh, I know." Jen held up a hand, and smiled. "I'm not trying to say anything about your care. I know he was safe, it's just…well, sometimes it's hard for me to remember that he's growing up."

Lisa nodded again, even though she couldn't possibly know what it was like to have a son who was growing up.

After Kayden disappeared through the door, Jen turned to her and suddenly she got nervous. What if Jen had heard about her reputation and that was what turned Jason off her? Was Jen going to confront her? If the ground could have opened up to swallow her, Lisa would have welcomed it at that moment.

"I wanted to thank you again."

"What?" The question popped out before she could stop it.

If Jen was surprised by her outburst, she didn't show it. She smiled. "I know I already thanked you for taking care of Kayden, but I really wanted to thank you for something else."

Confusion clouded her head, and she knew it showed on her face, but she couldn't help it. "I don't understand."

"I want to thank you for waking up my brother."

"Jason?"

Jen laughed and nodded. "That's the one. He's been living in kind of a fog for the last few years, and it's been a long time since I've seen him as happy as I did when you guys came down the mountain. I'm pretty sure I have you to thank for that."

As fast as the good feeling came, it went as Lisa remembered the way Jason's attitude had changed and the way he looked at her the last time they'd spoken, only hours earlier. "Well…" Lisa paused as she tried to decide how much to say to Jen. Finally she sighed, and continued. What did she have to lose? "He sure doesn't seem too happy with me anymore. So I don't know what to tell you."

Jen waved her hand and brushed away Lisa's concern. "Jason just needs to get out of his own way. And he will. Don't worry about that."

How did she not worry about that? Jason had all but told her to leave him alone. She wasn't going to pretend to understand it, but it had hurt nonetheless.

"I do want you to come to the Porter Party, though. I know it's a big family thing, and it has a ridiculous name." Jen shrugged. "Actually, the whole thing is ridiculous. But it's a lot of fun, and no matter what he says, he wants you there. He just doesn't know it yet."

"I don't know."

Jen grabbed her arm and forced her to look into her eyes. They were the identical deep green as Jason's and it was almost as if she stared at him. "Please," Jen said. "For me."

Before she could think of a suitable excuse, Lisa found herself nodding. "Okay," she said. "I'll be there."

Chapter Nine

USUALLY LISA LIKED any excuse to dress up and go to a party. There weren't a lot of opportunities at Castle Mountain Lodge, so she tended to jump at them. But as she prepared for the Porter Party, pulled her hair up into a simple but elegant twist and added a swipe of lip gloss, she felt like a black cloud hung over her. The second she'd agreed to the party, she'd regretted it. But seeing how pleased Jen was when she'd said yes, Lisa didn't have the heart to go back on her word. Besides, it wouldn't be all for nothing; she'd present the certificate to keep Ryan happy. But after that, she'd smile, say her goodbyes, and get out of there. She'd already tried to fix things with Jason, but she would not continue to bang her head against a brick wall. She could take a hint.

She slipped into a royal blue sheath dress that she knew complemented her eyes, grabbed her one pair of black pumps from the closet and stood back to admire the entire effect.

A smile played at her lips. She looked good. Damned good and she knew it. A part of her—a small part, but a part nonetheless—couldn't help but hope that Jason would see her and realize what he'd lost out on. It was childish, and she knew it, but the thought did help soothe her a little.

Before she could chicken out, Lisa grabbed her clutch that already held the gift certificate Ryan had prepared, as well as a few words he wanted her to say about the Lodge, and how appreciative they were for choosing the Lodge for their family reunion, or something like that. Lisa was pretty sure she could think of something better to say, but then again, if she looked at Jason, there was a very good chance that words would completely escape her. It didn't matter.

"Get in and get out, Lisa," she said to herself. She took one last look in the mirror, pasted on a smile, and left for the party.

The annual Porter Party was in full swing and even Jason had to admit, it wasn't totally lame, which probably had something to do with the event planning company the Lodge used to make the event a success. All the relatives were having fun: the older ones danced with the kids, and everyone else seemed to be laughing, drinking, and eating too much. All signs of a successful party. Everyone was having fun, except for Jason.

He'd spent the better part of the evening so far pacing the room, wishing he'd had the nerve to invite Lisa. Any event would be more fun with Lisa there. But even if he had asked her, there was no way she would come. He'd been a total jerk. Not once, not twice, but more times than even he could count. And what was worse was that his sister had nailed it on the head when she'd told him that Lisa wasn't Nikki, and he needed to smarten up or lose what could very possibly be the best thing that had happened to him in a long time.

Jen was right. Jen was always right. And there was no point in him hanging around the party thinking about it; he needed to fix things. If they could be fixed. He put his drink down on a nearby table and was just about to march out of the room, when a small group of his cousins stopped him.

"Don't be mad." Emily held out her hands in a peace gesture and flashed a smile that had Jason concerned. Very concerned.

"About what?" He scanned the faces of the others. Chase had a huge grin and nodded; Nolan, Emily's husband, looked slightly confused, but his arm was around his wife, and Jason knew he'd go along with anything. It was Conrad that Jason's eyes stopped at. He did not look happy. Not at all.

"He's not going to be mad, Em." Nolan rubbed her back. "It's not like he could keep it a secret forever."

"What?" Jason looked around the group again. He grew more and more confused.

"As if you didn't know," Conrad spat. "Were you planning on telling anyone, or were you just going to waltz into the office and take a seat at the head of the table?"

Oh. *That.* Realization filled Jason and he glanced at Emily, who at least looked sheepish. "I'm sorry, Jason. I didn't mean to say anything, but it kind of slipped out."

"It's okay."

"I think it's great." Chase slapped Jason on the back. "I know your dad's looking at retiring, and with you finally coming on board, it will finally be a true family business. Emily says you're probably going to work in operations and acquisitions."

"Did she now?" He narrowed his eyes at his favorite cousin, but he wasn't mad. Not really. It wasn't exactly the way he hoped to tell his family about his decision. A decision he himself hadn't been very sure of until that moment, but it seemed as good of a time as any. "The truth is, I'm not exactly sure what my role will be, but yes, I'll likely take over a lot of what Dad is doing so he can retire. It's time."

"Damn straight it is." Chase clapped him on the back again.

"I think we could have had a family vote on it."

"Oh, stuff it, Conrad." Jen came up beside Jason and gave him a supportive wink. "It's a family business—there's no voting. Otherwise we would have voted you out a long time ago."

Everyone laughed, and Conrad had the decency to look embarrassed. He said something else, but Jason didn't hear it. His eyes, and his attention, had been snagged by a vision in blue. He watched, sure his mouth hung open, as Lisa made her way through the room. Some of the men stopped to stare at her as she passed, no doubt taken off guard by her beauty and ease. She smiled and nodded at everyone as she made her way to the front of the room.

He had no idea why she was there, but he was determined to find out. Jason opened and closed his mouth, and was just about to excuse himself when Conrad spoke.

"I knew she'd come."

Jason flipped around, fists already curled at his sides. Conrad held his hands up in defense. "Not for me. For you."

"What?" Conrad's words were so unexpected, Jason wasn't sure he heard him properly.

"I'm not the enemy, Jason. What happened with…well, it wasn't planned and—"

"Don't." Jason shook his head. He didn't want to hear it. Not in front of everyone. "I don't think this is the time."

"I think it is," Conrad said. "I think it's way past time." His cousin took a step toward him and everyone else seemed to step back to make room for him. "I blame myself every day for what happened, Jason. It was my fault she was on the road that night and…I loved her, Jason. I'm sorry it went down the way it did." Conrad took a deep breath, and Jason saw the hurt lining his cousin's face. "I miss her every day."

Obviously finished saying his piece, Conrad exhaled long and low before adding one last thing. "I'm sorry," he said. "I'm so sorry." He turned and walked away, and Jason let him go. It would take a bit of time to process everything he'd just heard, but he knew he'd forgive his cousin. It was time, and there was obviously a lot more he didn't know.

He couldn't blame Conrad forever. It was just as much her fault as it was his. And more than that, Jason couldn't continue to live the way he was, untrusting of anyone he got close to. It was time to move on.

His eyes locked on Lisa's across the room. She stared at him, and even from a distance, Jason could see the realization there. He'd never told her who Nikki had deceived her with, but it was clear she'd somehow pieced everything together. She smiled ever so slightly in invitation and Jason didn't need to be asked twice. He left his cousins, who were likely still trying to process everything they'd just heard, behind, and with a single-minded determination crossed the room until he stood in front of her.

With her high heels on, she was almost as tall as he was, and he looked straight into her eyes. Given everything that had happened between them, he had no right to touch her, and she had every right to push him away when he put one hand on her narrow waist and cupped the back of her head with the other.

But she didn't. And when he pulled her close, close enough to smell the sweetness of the champagne she must have drunk earlier, she still didn't push him back.

"I'm supposed to present your sister with a gift certificate as a present from the Lodge."

So that's why she was there? He didn't care.

"Later," he whispered. "Now I need to talk."

She nodded slightly, and didn't take her eyes from his.

"I've been such a jerk." He spoke softly so only she could

hear. "I probably don't deserve it, but I'm hoping for it. Will you give me another chance?"

Lisa's nod was slight, but it was the touch of her lips on his that told him everything would be okay. He let her lead; his lips molded to the soft pressure she provided, while his thumb smoothed circles on her cheek. So lost in this woman who drove him crazy, he didn't even notice that his entire family surrounded them, likely taking in every second of the show they provided.

Lisa pulled back. She offered him a smile. "We have a lot to talk about, don't we?"

Jason nodded. He didn't even want to think about the logistics of how he'd make things work with her; all he knew was he would. No matter what. "And we will. But for now, let's dance."

He held out his hand, which she took. His fingers squeezed hers as he led her to the middle of the room, where he pulled her in close again for a slow dance. At some point the music had started to play again, and he would be eternally grateful to whoever it was who had selected a ballad at that moment. For a few moments they didn't speak, just moved together to the rhythm.

Finally, Lisa broke the silence. "I heard a rumor you were going to take the job with your family company?"

"How did you—"

"Ladies' room." She smiled. "I may have overheard a little." She laughed and the sweet sound filled his ears. Now that he had her back in his arms, Jason didn't plan to ever let her go.

"That means I'll be even closer to come visit you," he said. "And I do plan on coming to visit. A lot."

Her smile faded slightly and she ducked her head. "Well, that's the thing…"

A million ways to finish the sentence flew through his head, but Jason forced himself not to jump to conclusions. "What's the thing?"

"I think I might be ready for a change myself. I've been thinking of putting in my notice and going back to the city."

"But you love it here."

"I love a lot of things." Her smile was back. "And I think there might be a few other things I'm falling in love with, as well." Without giving him a chance to respond, she closed the gap between them with another kiss, and Jason felt himself fall a little, too.

I hope you loved Tempting Gifts! There is nothing more romantic than Christmas as the Lodge and that's exactly what's coming up next! Ryan's the newest customer service manager at the Lodge and he's been watching all the love stories play out right in front of him. Maybe this season he'll be able to unwrap his own happy ending?
Find out in Holiday Gifts.
You can read a sneak peak of his story right after this...

And if you want even more romance...click HERE for an exclusive FREE novella that isn't available anywhere else!

Holiday Gifts

Please enjoy an excerpt from Holiday Gifts, the next in the Castle Mountain Lodge Series

The moment they walked through the sliding doors into the main reception area of Castle Mountain Lodge, Julie Pitts's nose was assaulted by a combination of apple cinnamon spice like mulled cider and the pungent aroma of pine needles. Fresh pine boughs hung from every available shelf and banister, a fire burned welcomingly in the stone hearth where felt stockings hung, and in the center of the huge vaulted room stood the largest Christmas tree Julie had ever seen.

It was as if everything clichéd and country Christmas was put in a bottle, shaken and dumped all over the room.

It was perfect.

"This is fantastic."

Julie turned to see her daughter, Shay, arms outstretched, taking in the room with a smile that she knew matched her own. "Right?"

"I'm so glad we came, Mom." Her daughter threw her arms around her in an impulsive hug. One Julie was only too happy to accept. At sixteen, public displays were fewer and further between than she would have liked. "It's going to be the best Christmas ever. How could it not, right?"

Julie smiled, but shook her head at Shay's childish enthusiasm. She was such a mixture of woman and child, it was hard to keep up some days, but she did have a point. "It's going to be fantastic," she agreed. "But first, we have work to do." She slipped out of her daughter's embrace and turned until she found the check-in desk. "Let's get settled. We have a big night ahead of us."

The whole purpose of the trip to the Lodge, and the only reason Julie could justify the expense of renting a private chalet suite for them, was because she was incorporating the holiday with business. Crafty Creations was only in its third year, but her idea of home crafting parties and women's retreats was becoming increasingly popular. A last-minute Christmas-themed retreat had been her daughter's idea and although it was a good one, Julie was fairly sure Shay had ulterior motives. *No*, she silently amended. *She was positive.*

Shay had been obsessed with spending Christmas at the Lodge ever since she heard about the elaborate Holly Berry Ball they held every year on Christmas Eve. Heck, Shay was obsessed with everything Christmas. Or at least she had been for the last few years. Ever since her father had remarried and started to spend the holidays exclusively with his *new family*. She tried to pretend as if it didn't matter, but Julie could see the hurt caused by her increasingly distant relationship with her father.

She took the key cards the front desk clerk handed her and looked over at her daughter, who was ladling herself a cup of apple cider from a drink station by the fireplace. Her daughter wanted the perfect Christmas, and that's exactly what Julie was going to give her. After everything they'd been through, she deserved it. Shay was a good kid. She really did deserve a good holiday season and it was long overdue that Julie gave it to her. She'd been so busy working for the last few years, trying to get her business up and running, and before then, working toward her degree in business while working full-time to support them. It was definitely time. Even if that meant mixing a little bit of work with their holiday.

"Are you ready to get started, Shay?"

"You have to try this, Mom." She held her cup of cider in the air. "It's unbelievable. It's like Christmas in a cup."

Julie laughed. Of course it was. This entire place was living and breathing Christmas. "I'll try some later. We have to get set up. We're running late." Julie felt a twinge of guilt rushing Shay, but it was true. They were running late. They had a very special destination theme Crafty Creations Corner set for later that evening. It was an overnight event where participants spent time crafting a variety of ornaments and greeting cards before enjoying all the amenities of the Lodge, followed by a festive brunch the next day. It was Shay's idea, and if it worked out, Julie planned to do a lot more of them. The event had sold out completely in only days and as long as there weren't any major issues, it would be a lucrative event.

As long as there weren't any major issues.

That was the one thing that had Julie concerned. Major issues. Like forgetting materials. Or even worse, crafting supplies. Worst-case scenario, if she forgot a few pom poms or buttons, Julie could improvise. But what she couldn't fake her way through was a lack of glue, or thread, or card stock. She'd double-checked and then checked her supply cart again. She had Shay count everything separately as well, and she planned enough extra supplies for five extra people. She didn't plan to have any drop-ins, but there were always at least one or two people who either didn't follow instructions or had perfectionist tendencies and wanted to start their project over. Julie had learned that lesson the hard way.

"You're sure you don't want some cider?" Shay shoved a paper cup in her mother's direction, but Julie only shook her head.

"I will," she said. "Later. I promise. I really want to go get set up and make sure there aren't any surprises."

Shay tossed back the rest of her drink, grabbed the luggage cart they'd loaded with their plastic tubs of supplies and dutifully pushed it alongside Julie down the hall.

"Mom, you know everything is going to be awesome, right?" Shay swerved the cart and jumped on it, riding it a little like a child down the corridor. "How could it not be? This place totally rocks. It's like a Christmas card."

Julie bit her lip to keep from chastising her. There probably wasn't any harm in riding the cart. "I know you're right, Shay. Um, maybe you..." She couldn't help herself. She had to say something. "No." She shook her head. "Never mind."

Shay laughed and gave the cart a shove, sending it ahead of her a few feet. "You're so up—oops."

The cart chose that moment to hit a bump in the tile floor. It careened into the wall, where it knocked over the precariously balanced stack of storage totes. Shay darted for it, but couldn't get to it in time to save the bin full of carefully sorted and separated card stock from tumbling off the top and crashing to the floor in a sea of paper.

"Oh, Shay! It was all—" Julie forced herself to take a breath. It wasn't a big deal. She couldn't get herself all worked up over card stock. No doubt there would be bigger challenges to face before the night was over.

"I'm so sorry, Mom." Her daughter pulled the paper together and tossed it back into the bin. "I promise I'll get it all sorted out before everything starts. You won't even know it was messed up. And even if you do, no one else will. I'll fix it."

Julie forced herself to take a deep breath and released it slowly. She laughed and shook her head. She really did need to learn a thing or two from her daughter. "It's fine. Besides, this is our room right here." She glanced down at the paper again and then the plaque over the door that marked it as Mt. Rundle. "We have two hours. Let's get everything set up."

As the events manager for Castle Mountain Lodge, Christmas was hands down the busiest time of the year for Ryan Morrison. Ever since he'd taken over the role at the mountain resort, he'd been busting his butt trying to fill the hole that Carmen Kincaid, the previous events manager, had left behind. According to most of the staff, and even some guests, at the hotel, she'd been amazing and when she'd moved on to the new resort, the Springs, with her new boyfriend, it had become Ryan's job to take over. He'd been doing his best, and finally after a few Christmas seasons under his belt, he'd found his groove. This year, he was more than ready for the events and special festivities that would take place.

Ryan scanned the lobby area and the decorations that had been carefully displayed. A talented pianist played soft holiday favorites at the grand piano in the corner of the room; the sounds floated over everything. The scent of cider hung in the air. It had been an added touch this year and one that was so well received, he'd planned to do it again. He'd also been thinking about working with the kitchen group to put together an eggnog station for Christmas Day as a little extra treat for the guests staying over the holiday.

Just like he was.

Alone.

Again.

The fact that Ryan was alone for the holidays yet again was the only thing that put a damper on his festive spirit. At thirty, he was ready to find someone to spend his life with. In all honesty, he'd been ready for years. Not that he admitted it for a long time. He was too busy trying to play it cool and be the swinging single guy like all his friends. He'd been playing a role. A role he didn't fit into at all. He'd never been the player type the way his childhood friends were. For the life of him, he couldn't see the appeal to dating multiple women and not settling down with one special woman. But he'd gone along with the crowd and tried to play their game. Unfortunately that meant falling into a rut that only perpetuated everything he didn't want. It was a vicious cycle and it took him way too long to realize he'd never get what he wanted by sticking around that crowd. It had been time to move on.

And that's what he'd done.

Only moving on meant taking a job at Castle Mountain Lodge, which had been fantastic and an amazing opportunity, career-wise. But it was hard to meet people, let alone a woman he wanted to marry, working in the tourism industry.

Ryan let out a long sigh and ran his fingers through his hair. There wasn't much to be done about it. Not for the time being anyway. Eventually he'd have to move on or accept the fact that maybe marriage just wasn't in the cards.

"Ryan?" Desiree, one of the new desk clerks they'd hired for the winter months, called to him, breaking him out of his woe-is-me cycle. It was probably a good thing. No, it was definitely a good thing

"Hey." He turned in her direction and tried to look as if he'd been paying attention to things. "What's up?"

"I need a break." She stuck her bottom lip out and batted her eyelashes. She was a gorgeous girl and no doubt, that technique definitely would have worked on some men. But for Ryan, it only made him shake his head. "It's *so* busy, Ryan. And I really need to use the little girls' room."

He glanced at his watch. "Your break isn't for another two hours, Des. You'll be okay."

"But I really have to go." She all but stamped her foot and he would have just walked away, but then she added, "It's a *girl* thing."

Dammit. That was practically impossible to argue. It wasn't his job to cover her station and he had every right to say no and lodge a complaint with her boss. But what was the point? "Fine. I'll watch the desk for five minutes. But I have things to do, so hurry back, okay?"

Her face transformed with a smile and she jetted off in the direction of the bathroom without a second glance. All he could do was shake his head after her. It's not that all the women who worked at the Lodge were ditzy airheads like Desiree, who used their charm—or in Des's case, her looks—to get what they wanted. But some definitely were. The other women he'd met had rules about getting involved with people they worked with, or weren't his type.

No. He definitely wasn't going to find the woman of his dreams working at the Lodge. It was a thought that saddened him every time he allowed it to enter his thoughts. But he was going to have to deal with it. A choice would have to be made.

"In the New Year," he muttered under his breath.

"Pardon?" Ryan glanced up to see a young woman in front of him, a look of confusion and amusement on her pretty face. "Were you talking to me about the New Year?" she asked. "Because if you were, I'm probably not going to be here for the New Year. But maybe I'll come back next year. If that's what you were talking about. But if you were trying to tell me that something is going to happen in the—"

"No," he interrupted her, completely amused by the girl in front of him. "I was just talking to myself. Sorry." And it was Ryan who was sorry, sorry that he hadn't let her continue her monologue. It was the most entertainment he'd had all day.

She smiled and tossed her long dark hair over her shoulder. "It's fine. But if you have some sort of problem with the New

Year, I'm more than happy to help you with it. In fact, I'm a pretty good problem solver. Is there something you have a problem with?"

He laughed. "Not at all." She was definitely entertaining. If a little young. It was too bad, really. The most interesting person he'd run across in days, weeks maybe, and she was clearly way too young for him. He shook his head. "In fact," he said, "it's my job to help you. What can I do for you?"

"My name is Shay." She straightened her shoulders and stood at attention. "I'm here with Crafty Creations and we're in the Mt. Rundle room."

"That's right." He remembered that booking. It seemed as though it might be a good offering for their guests, plus the woman in charge had pre-registered participants, who'd also booked rooms. It was a win-win for the Lodge and Ryan was interested to see how it would work out. If it was successful, he definitely wanted to look into offering it in the future for other seasons as well. "I remember that," he said. "I hope the room is working out for you."

"It is," Shay said officially. "Except we can't get the speakers to work."

"Speakers?" He tipped his head.

"Yeah, you know." The girl waved her arms in elaborate gestures. "You plug them in and they play music. It's a *really* new technology." Her voice dripped with the sarcasm that only teenagers could pull off. "Speakers."

"Right." He nodded his head elaborately. "I have actually heard of them. You can adjust them so they play music at different volumes, right?"

She rolled her eyes, but her lips twitched in a smile.

"I think I can help you, Shay." Ryan laughed. "There are speakers in the room, but they probably forgot to put an audio cable in there. Let me find someone who can fix that for you." He took a quick sweep of the room, but only saw Desiree making her way, rather slowly, from the bathroom. "You know what?" He made a quick decision. "I think I can help you with that myself." He waved Desiree over, who looked less than happy for her un-scheduled break to be done so quickly, and gestured to Shay to follow him. "Come with me. We'll get you all set up."

It only took a minute for him to get the audio cable out of the storage cupboard and after some more friendly banter with the young girl, they made their way down the corridor to the Mt. Rundle room where the craft night was to take place.

"So." Shay gave Ryan an appraising look. "Are you single?"

"Pardon me?" He almost tripped on the carpet in the hall. "Why do you need to know that?"

"Duh." She rolled her eyes. "It's kind of the question you ask when you're interested in someone."

"Interested?" *Interested?* She was a cute kid and maybe if she was ten or fifteen years older he'd be interested. But she wasn't. So there was no point even thinking about it. That would make him some sort of sicko and Ryan was definitely not in the business of being any kind of creeper. *No.* Shay definitely had the wrong idea. "You shouldn't be interested in me. I'm way too old for you."

She laughed so hard that she doubled over with laughter and he had to stop and wait for her before they could continue. Shay carried on for what seemed like hours before she finally straightened herself, wiping the tears from her eyes and adjusting her hair.

"Are you going to be okay?" Ryan had to restrain himself from rolling his eyes. It wasn't *that* funny.

"I'm fine," she managed. They started to walk again. "And for the record, you are way too old for me." He was about to say something, but before he could, she added, "But it's too bad really. I'm a lot of fun." She winked. "And I'm pretty cute, too. If only there was an older version of me, right?"

Ryan couldn't help it. This girl had just verbalized exactly what he'd been thinking almost from the moment he'd met her. If there was an older version of her…funny, beautiful, obviously witty and smart, well…

"Here we are." Shay ran ahead and pushed open the door to the room. "I got a cable," she called out. "And a man!"

Ryan laughed and looked at his feet, shaking his head. She really was a piece of work. When he looked up again, his breath caught in his throat. The woman who looked like just that—an older version of Shay—stood at the front of the room, holding some sort of craft project in her hand. The younger girl's words replayed like a flash through his brain. *If only there was an older version of me.*

Will Shay's plan of playing matchmaker this Christmas work? Find out and read the rest of Holiday Gifts now!

About the Author

Elena Aitken is a USA Today Bestselling Author of more than forty romance and women's fiction novels. The mother of 'grown up' twins, Elena now lives with her very own mountain man in the heart of the very mountains she writes about. She can often be found with her toes in the lake and a glass of wine in her hand, dreaming up her next book and working on her own happily ever after.

To learn more about Elena:
www.elenaaitken.com
elena@elenaaitken.com

www.ingramcontent.com/pod-product-compliance
Lightning Source LLC
LaVergne TN
LVHW051006080826
845145LV00009B/2480

* 9 7 8 1 9 2 7 9 6 8 7 5 8 *